THE BISHOP'S VILLA

Sacha Naspini

THE BISHOP'S VILLA

*Translated from the Italian
by Clarissa Botsford*

Europa
editions

Europa Editions
27 Union Square West, Suite 302
New York NY 10003
www.europaeditions.com
info@europaeditions.com

Copyright © 2023 by Edizioni e/o
First publication 2024 by Europa Editions

Translation by Clarissa Botsford
Original title: *Villa del seminario*
Translation copyright © 2024 by Europa Editions

Library of Congress Cataloging in Publication Data is available
ISBN 979-8-88966-052-1

Naspini, Sacha
The Bishop's Villa

Cover design and illustration by Ginevra Rapisardi

Prepress by Grafica Punto Print – Rome

Printed in Canada

C O N T E N T S

SETTEBELLO - 13

DEAR ANNA - 71

THE BISHOP'S VILLA - 97

IN THE THICK - 153

TWENTY YEARS LATER - 191

AUTHOR'S NOTE - 211

ABOUT THE AUTHOR - 217

To Edith

THE BISHOP'S
VILLA

SETTEBELLO

1.

He thought back to when the circus came to Le Case in '37: camels and dromedaries on a leash, beasts he'd heard about since he was a kid, and there they were, their pelts and maws buzzing with flies.

The creatures he was looking at now were another matter. For one thing, they were no different to him or the other townsfolk, except that they looked like they'd given up the ghost. They resembled grazing sheep, one guard in front and another in the rear. But they soon fell out of line; the soldiers were just boys and, as such, were looking for fun, with a tipple here and a smile from a girl there. That mongrel who'd been lodged in town for months was with them. René saw him slip into Barbarina's house. Nobody took any notice.

In the meantime, the prisoners were going into stores and handing over lists of supplies to take back to the villa. It was a chance to stretch their legs and get an hour of air, but their job was no better than a mule's. Once they'd picked up the packages and cans, they re-grouped in front of St. Bastian's, waiting for their guards' R&R to end. Then it was, "Hop along! Move, move!" and they shouldered their loads and set off along Via di Mezzo in single file, heads down. Some people in town closed their shutters as they went by, in a show of either aversion or obedience.

A harsh winter was on its way; it was only November and they were already shaking like mice. Spring felt so far away that thinking about it was like imagining a different life. Old ladies with no families would wrap up in blankets to go and collect their rations; staying upright, holding onto the wall as they went, was a miracle. If they slipped on a sheet of ice and broke their knee, they would tell their rescuers not to bother, they were as good as dead anyway. A few days before, René had been the one to help Stella Fantastici up from the sidewalk. She had murmured, "Mario was so good-looking," and had then gone quiet. Disoriented by the shattered hip, she was clinging to the mental picture of her long-dead husband. Shocks of this kind are all that remained of life. Stella was now bed-ridden, with a son fighting a war and no husband. She was unlikely to live until Christmas, never mind Easter.

When the women prisoners were brought into town, it was evident that, unlike the men, they had no chores, except to stay in line, with Leonilde Cacciaferri letting loose if she happened to catch one of them dawdling in front of the store windows. "That stuff is not for the likes of you!" she would shriek, waving her whip in the air. She enjoyed making these scenes: it established her position in the pecking order, the responsibility she had been given thanks to her father's sucking up to the mayor. It was a role she'd taken to right from the start, as if she'd been born to yell at those poor wretches. It was true, they were more defiant than the men: they didn't hang their heads if they ever made eye-contact with people in town. If anything, they seemed to be looking for a challenge, even the two young girls. Those dark eyes like headlights would shoot looks which meant, "This is what they're doing to us. And you're just standing there." In the end, it was the locals who had to look away, as if the women's plight had stripped their souls bare.

René felt the daggers in their looks, too. But what could he do? Everywhere there was fear, poverty, rationing, the worry when your loved ones didn't return from the front or from hideouts in the woods. The freezing cold didn't help. In fact, it crooned a horrible tune that left everyone with one question: how many of them would ever get to hear the end of it? Old people were perishing little by little and turning to dust. Once the ghost of starvation got into your bones, you turned into a brute. Other people's problems became irrelevant; the only thing that mattered was finding a way to put a bowl of gruel on the table for your little one's supper. You started despising people worse off than you. That air of superiority a pauper displayed when someone even more impoverished came along. That's how desperate people got their revenge. News of a prison camp just outside town might even have made some people feel better.

In the early days, people wondered, "How can this happen here in Maremma?" Le Case had always been a nowhere town lost in some nowhere mountains. Its only saving grace was that it looked down on the open sewer of the marshes, where malaria still lurked in the brackish water. Further down, right on the horizon, there was the sea, but only on clear days, which between October and May you could count on the fingers of one hand. As if it were jeering, "Look, you nasty people, the world exists. But it's not for the likes of you!" Just like Leonilde with her prisoners when they glanced at a store window.

Even the war looked different from up there—it was wrapped in a cloak of waiting and praying. The action was almost always somewhere else; nothing ever bothered to make its way up the mountain, with all those hairpin bends. Then, boom! There was a rope team of underdogs. All of a sudden, things started happening that, a moment before, would only ever have taken place on another planet.

The Fascists were quick to respond. Take Claudio Montalti, or Mandela as he was known in town. He had taken to going out clean-shaven in his Sunday best, even though he might catch his death of cold, just in case new military units arrived. Mothers had started primping their daughters' hair to make them look marriageable. Pathetic little men were getting horny at the prospect of fresh opportunities and running over to the garrison to offer Maresciallo Rizziello their services.

In general, it was as if every townsperson had taken in a guest who did nothing but stand in a corner. Staring in silence. Only a few days earlier, nobody had paid much attention to the bishop's residence, where His Holiness's limbs had always sought refuge from the humidity that strangled Grosseto over the summer. Monsignor Galeazzi was holed up in his villa at that moment, staying well clear of the tragedy of the evacuees following the air-raids. Now, however, news from the villa was rumbling in people's ears like thunder. As a consequence, people played dumb, even when their breath suddenly caught in their throats as they said good morning.

2

W e know how things are," Anna said, dunking a piece of bread in her warmed-up wine. "Boscaglia says that pig Ercolani wants to distinguish himself and advance his career."

René shot a glance at the window: whenever he came into the house these days, he felt under siege, even though all they did was talk. "He's been elected governor of the province," he said. "What more does he want?"

She shuddered, as if the devil had lain a hand on her shoulder. "He's always looking for something, that's for sure. Meanwhile, he's appointed Rizziello to run the camp."

"Everyone knows that."

"He's the one that drafted the rental contract."

René thought it was absurd. "Ercolani asked to rent the villa? You mean they didn't just requisition it?"

"Guess who signed the agreement?"

"Who?"

"Monsignor Galeazzi."

"The bishop himself?"

"In person."

"Maybe he had no idea what—"

"Five thousand lira a month, plus a salary for the nuns and two workers. Boscaglia says their brigade managed to get their hands on an unofficial copy and it mentions a bishop 'motivated by the emergency of war.' And get this: 'proof of a special tribute to the new government . . .'" Anna cleared her throat. "May peace be with them."

René was perplexed. "Can he do it?"

"Worse. He already has."

On his way upstairs, he thought about what he had learned. He was by no means tied to a priest's tunic like some people were, but that shameful news still felt like a dreadful betrayal, and God had a hand in it. He thought about Anna, too, and how it was eating at her heart. After Edoardo's death, the Resistance was the only thing stopping her from going mad. She had to carry on the battle for her son, who had been executed by the Wehrmacht. René could still see the three military police officers who had come to her door with the news. Her wails could be heard up the stairwell at night. Sobs that were impossible to stifle. He would sometimes go downstairs and let himself in using the key Anna insisted on keeping between two stones on the ground, where the plaster had peeled away years before. She had always left it there in case handsome Edoardo needed to come back on the sly. René would find her sitting at the kitchen table, a little tipsy. She wasn't even surprised when he appeared. She would stare at him as if he were made of air. Words served no purpose. Holding the bony hand of a mortally-wounded mother served no purpose. Anna had moved to the edge of another world, and everything around her, she herself, had turned to mist. René's skin would crawl when she started talking like a child, her nose running, the snot blending with her tears. She would stare into space and speak to her boy, as if he were right there in front of her. "Have you eaten?" she would ask. "I've put a bed-warmer in for you . . . " Exhausted by the pain, she would fade and start flickering like a dying candle. Her words slowed down and, little by little, her eyelids would begin to droop. René would leave her asleep at the table after draping a blanket over her shoulders.

There were other nights when he would be consumed by curiosity and lie on the floor of his apartment upstairs with a glass to his ear. He could sometimes make out footsteps. And what sounded like voices. But he never knew whether he was making it all up.

He didn't ask and she didn't want to talk about it. God only knew what strategems Anna used to communicate with the partisans, but there were times when René struggled to reason with her. "You know what would happen if . . . "

Anna wouldn't let him finish. She would get up and busy herself with something, or change the subject. But she wasn't jeopardizing only herself. If the Germans ever heard there was a direct line to a partisan brigade in that building, all of them would be led, hands tied, to the edge of the bluff where a bust of Chancellor Ferrer once stood, and be shoved off with a gunshot in the back. Anna, himself, and the Calò family on the top floor.

Patrols around Le Case had always been half-hearted, but the business at the villa had been a game-changer. Ercolani had sent the military police and an extra twenty soldiers to Rizziello to help keep an eye on the camp. While it was impossible to dissuade his desperate friend from communicating with the brigade, René could at least try to rein in any of her excesses. Otherwise, the partisans might get the idea that they had found the perfect base for their incursions. Taking advantage of a distraught mother willing to do anything to avenge her son's death would be a piece of cake.

He also kept tabs on the new recruits escorting the prisoners on their errands. A rookie he'd never seen before had turned up at his workshop the other day. No older than twenty-three, he had a strange accent: southern maybe, or a medley of dialects he'd picked up since leaving home. The young soldier couldn't believe the jackpot he'd won. He'd never had to do so little as he did in this posting. Out of the blue, he'd said, "Hey, Pops, do you know where I can find a nest for my pecker?"

René had been happily taking boots tied together with their laces out of the sack the soldier had been carrying, until he had lined up three pairs on the counter, together with a pair of sturdy women's shoes with a hole in the sole. "Sorry, what was that?" he said, thinking of the money he'd be making.

"Cooch. Pussy . . . what do you call it here?"

"Well, we have some nice girls here, no doubt."

The soldier was keen to explore the matter further. "Do they give head?"

"Sorry?"

The soldier stuck his thumb in his mouth and mimed a gulp of wine from a flask. Then he popped his thumb out, making the sound of a bottle being uncorked. "I mean, when the chick pecks, does she swallow the cock chowder?"

"Ah, that," René spluttered. "I don't . . . "

The soldier was amped up and might well have had a drink or two, though it was still morning. He caught sight of Rene's hand. The right one. "Tell me about it. My father's the same."

René's instinct was to hide it in his pocket or behind his back, as he always did in front of other people. "A lathe. I was twelve."

"So, no war, right?"

"No war."

The soldier was young, but there was already a martial air about him; he took two steps forward and grabbed René's wrist. He stood there for a while, staring at the mangled hand, turning it slightly towards the light. He saw the stubs of the middle, ring and little fingers. "Hard to hold a rifle with these," he muttered. "Hard to do anything," he added, the implication being that working with hammers, pincers and plyers must be equally difficult. Then he dropped the hand with an expression of disgust.

He handed René the delivery receipt, informed him that someone would be picking up the footwear, and dashed to the door. Before leaving, he turned and said, "You never answered my question, Pops."

René's gaze fell involuntarily on the leather-cutting shears by the cash register. He smiled. "What was the question again?"

"How do you call it around here?"

René just stood there. The young soldier was in a hurry so he brought the conversation to an abrupt end. "Okay then, I'll ask around."

A second later, he heard the door slam.

3.

Sometimes he would dream he had a whole hand that could pick things up, point, or count to ten. When he woke up, he would linger in bed for a few minutes, phantom fingers under the covers bringing back memories and sensations from a long-lost time when his right hand was complete. He would rub the fingertips against the sheet, the rough cotton chafing a ring finger and a pinkie. Riding this fervid dream, he could even feel a fingernail scratching at the thin material.

The perception of having a fully-working hand would continue even after he was fully awake. In the bathroom, the soap bar would slip out of his grip, or when he picked up a matchbox, it would fall onto the stove, as if a hole had opened up in his palm. "Settebello, what's wrong?" he would mumble, almost amused.

People in Le Case knew him by the name of the winning card in scopa: the seven of coins. Even in peace time, the town never let you off the hook: too much or too little of anything soon became your cross to bear. Divo: a sobriquet for the man who would have liked to be an actor but had spent his life sweltering in the belly of a mine. Bandierina was what they called Nenni's son after he had been hit by a flagpole at the donkey race of '29—ten days in hospital, from which he returned irremediably retarded. There were others: Bretella, Meraviglia, Volevo, Ramengo, Domani. The primer of women's monikers was just as long, but their names usually alluded to something ghoulish or lascivious. For example, Colletta was known as the

Arch-Harpy of Montemassi, whereas Leonilde Cacciaferri, who had recently been seen brandishing an ash whip, was known as the Black Widow.

Battle names in a petty war, where any ambition was punished, any defect embellished. In that circus of strange animals, seven-fingered René had been christened Settebello, after the seven of coins card, and no one from outside town would ever have dreamed of asking why.

As soon as they came through the door of the Due Porte bar, the old men would guffaw while greeting him with jokes about the game of Scopa and his missing fingers.

He would always play along. Showing any weakness when teased was a mistake he had learned to avoid when he was a kid. The repercussions could be terrible; a long face would be repaid, with interest. But there were times when he would come home feeling first bitter, then resentful, and eventually angry. There had been some particularly bad days, especially when he was younger, when he had contemplated cutting off one more finger just to screw the town. Just to bait them. What nickname would they be able to saddle him with that played on the number six?

He had seen his classmates go off to war, never to return. The truth was, at the end of the day, the accident at the lathe may actually have saved his life. And yet he felt cheated: discarded, rejected in every way, from firing a rifle to walking up the aisle. René was neither handsome nor ugly. There were people with goat-brains and stuck-in-the-mud hearts who had raised a family and whose nerves were shot because they had a son at the Russian front or wherever. He had never had any of these experiences. His affections had been unrequited from the very beginning, when the neighborhood kids called him Pistola and would all experiment with a little groping and petting with Dora Palmieri behind the rocks at San Martino. Love had the same value in Le Case as anywhere else, but net-worth trumped everything. A clean bill of health, in mind and body, was also a pre-requisite. You had to pass all these tests before looks and feelings were taken into account. A husband who struggled to carry two buckets at a time was out of the question. Not to mention the revulsion at being touched by stubs, which was among other things a harbinger of bad luck.

People probably said, "René will always be René." The cripple who somehow managed to work with awls, presses and boar-hair brushes in the family workshop. Who replaced soles and fixed heels. Who would step outside every now and again to smoke a cigarette and watch the comings and goings in the street. He was such a permanent fixture that people had stopped noticing him.

It was December 7 when he went down to Anna's house at the usual time and found a surprise. On the table was a half-pan of castagnaccio, a chestnut-flour cake with extra walnuts and orange rind; beside it, a freshly-opened flask of wine.

"I haven't forgotten!" she said, inviting him to sit down.

René wasn't used to being shown kindness and, when it happened, he never knew what to say. He mumbled, "You're crazy, you shouldn't have . . . ". Times were hard enough; some people had to count the crumbs on the table and keep some back for the next day. Putting on such a lavish display at five o'clock in the afternoon felt rash.

"Don't be silly," she said, filling his glass. "Speaking of which, how many happy returns?" It didn't sound like a real question.

René allowed himself a chuckle. "Fifty. A round number."

"Wow! Half a century!"

"Saying it like that gives me a heart attack . . . "

"Come here." Anna stretched her arm across the table and clinked her friend's glass.

Moments like this made him think that there could have

been something more between the two of them. Loneliness for loneliness, it might have been possible to build a life together. She, the seamstress and he, the cobbler. Years before, after Carlo died, she had been left to cope alone: a young wife with a baby boy. René used to invent little tasks for young Edoardo, who spent a lot of time in his workshop. He would show him his tools and let him fool around with balls of glue. He had practically adopted the boy, and his affection had been returned. Once he started school, Edoardo would come in armed with a notebook and clear a corner of the counter for his homework. Without a family of his own, René had plans: to teach the boy the secrets of his trade and when the time came, hand the business over to him. Needless to say, when the military police came to the front door to give Anna the news, the tremors were felt upstairs, too.

They ate the castagnaccio without a word. It was a special feast and, as such, was to be enjoyed in religious silence. At a certain point, she started talking, without looking up from her plate. "Boscaglia says there have been more arrivals."

René felt his blood fizz. "You mean—?"

"They're bussing them in from Pitigliano and from Amiata. Many of them were imprisoned in Santa Fiora before. Did you see what the circular said?"

He nodded.

Anna wasn't satisfied. "And?"

René struggled to find words. He would have loved to mouth off about the terrible things being done to entire families—the old, the sick, and the children—who had been stripped of their possessions and rounded up. On the other hand, venting might set Anna off, which was to be avoided. Without taking into account another fact: the prison camp was not only a magnet for soldiers; it was bound to attract partisans as well. The amount of information Anna had received recently was proof. He imagined the resistance fighters huddling together in the woods, weaving webs like spiders. He parried her question with, "If I were a priest, I would be praying for them."

Anna made a face and burst out laughing. "What's the point of praying?" She knocked back her drink indignantly. Finally, she said, "Listen, we need to do something."

"Like?"

Anna stood up and started pacing around the table. "I don't know. For example, we know they have ringed the camp with barbed wire, which is one thing. There are four sentry towers manned with machine guns day and night. We know that—"

It was too much for René. "We know?" he blurted. "Anna, do me a favor. Sit down, and stop talking like a—"

She countered, "Like a—?"

René took a deep breath. He completed the sentence in a different tone: "For the love of God, you are not a partisan."

Anna flinched as though he had hit a nerve. She would have more readily accepted being called a whore. She puffed out her chest in defiance. "Who says?"

They had never gone this far. René looked out of the window, as if partisans and soldiers were standing outside eavesdropping on their argument. He needed to get rid of the card he was holding and decided to bet everything he had on it. "You wouldn't do it if Edoardo were still here."

She looked as though she had been slapped. Or as though what he'd said was double Dutch. "Excuse me?"

René had no choice but to stick to his guns, even though he was already regretting it. "Come on, be honest."

All of a sudden, the energy drained out of Anna. She fell like a dead weight into her chair. Then she picked up the flask and poured herself a generous glass of wine, which she sipped slowly as she looked at her friend. Her eyes were glistening.

Opposite her, sat a man who was just as upset. René should never have dumped that card, especially after a birthday feast in his honor. But it was on the table now. "Anna, forget it.

Edoardo would be the first to tell you to carry on," he mumbled, his heart on his sleeve.

She took in what he was saying. Then, her gaze darted around the room without landing anywhere in particular. A shadow of a smile flitted across her face. "You've said it twice."

"What?"

"His name."

René was knocked sideways but forced himself to take back control. "Forget the brigade, the prison camp, all of it. None of it will turn the clocks back."

Incredibly, she nodded. She even reached out her hand. Almost in a whisper, she said, "Boscaglia is convinced and I believe him. There's only one way to get over grief."

"Which is?"

"Finding purpose."

René grew animated. "But I'm here, I'm ready to—"

Anna smiled. "The people who took away my future are giving me another chance."

4.

On opening the front door of the building, he was dazzled by the whiteness. Just up the road, an army van had run adrift and soldiers were laying down planks to gain traction. Old Dorina from the building opposite was lowering a basket from the second floor for someone to fill it with firewood. People were busy shoveling their store fronts, as René would soon be doing. The children were the only ones who looked happy with their snowball fights in the middle of the road.

It wasn't the first time he and Anna had fought. Every now and again they would have arguments that drove them apart. It had nearly always been Anna who made the first move. She would come to the landing a couple of hours later with an herb omelet. They wouldn't need to overdo it with apologies to settle things. But this time was different. Three days after parting ways René had seen no sign of her.

In the meantime, Le Case had changed, as had its inhabitants: their expressions were dark, dread smoldering behind their eyes. The blizzard was partly to blame, of course; with that much snow, everything had come to a halt and even stepping out to fetch milk was unimaginable. But there was something else. Making his way past huddled groups, he caught a few snippets of alarming conversation. It seemed there had been a skirmish with the partisans that night. The storm had brought them out into the open like hungry wolves. A few shots had been fired near the villa. There had been no fatalities.

It was a miserable morning; the minutes marched by like an army of sleepwalkers. By midday, René realized there would be no orders coming in, but he forced himself to hold on a little longer. He waited until the bells of St. Bastian's struck three before preparing to leave. As he stepped outside, he felt the shock of icy air on his face.

The street was deserted at that hour. After their initial excitement, all the kids had been called back in lest they caught their deaths of cold. Although it was still early, the sky looked ready to close for the night. René moved cautiously; one wrong step and, in a matter of seconds, he would be keeping Stella Fantastici company with a broken hip.

He reached the front door of his building. Extracting his key was difficult enough; his good hand felt detached from his body. In the end, he managed to get it open. He stomped his feet to free his boots of the blocks of ice that had formed around them, and stepped inside.

He had intended to slip upstairs and forget everything, but he paused in the hall and looked at his friend's door. He made up his mind then and there: he would rather declare defeat than live with the tormenting presence of a broken tooth. "What are we doing?" he muttered to himself. "Life is hard enough as it is . . . " And anyway, how was Anna coping with the snow? Did she need anything? René thought it would be a good idea to ring on the door and say something like, "Are you going to make me a little omelet or what?" He didn't give it another thought.

Three light knocks echoed around the landing. That was usually enough. But Anna didn't come to the door.

"Maybe she's in the bathroom," he said, and knocked again. Nothing.

There was no way his friend had ventured out; she hadn't done so for weeks. In this weather, it was even less likely.

He knocked again, this time calling out, "Anna, are you there?"

His heart started thumping. After laying his ear on the door, hoping to intercept the clacking of her house shoes, he didn't waste another second. He crouched down, grabbed the secret key hidden between the stones, and opened the door.

It was pitch dark inside. René felt for the light switch on the wall to the left of the door. Once the light went on in the corridor, he was even more scared: there was not a soul in sight. He pictured her on the bed having died of heartbreak, collapsed in the kitchen, or bleeding from the forehead in the bathroom. The palpitations were scrambling his thoughts. "Hey," he called out, in little more than a whisper. He advanced into the house as if he were venturing into a wolf's den.

He went over what he would say to Dr. Salghini. "Emilio, I found her here. She looks like she's sleeping, doesn't she?" He reached the the kitchen. The light switch was stiff.

Again, no trace of Anna. Then he saw the table. The last time he'd been there, there'd been a half-tray of castagnaccio, a flask of wine, and two glasses. Now there was something else.

A cookie tin.

A sheet of paper.

So, these are her memoirs, he said to himself. The idea that Anna had killed herself in one of the rooms (but how?) made him take a step back. Best not touch anything. Or had she gone and thrown herself down one of the creeks? Le Case was obliging that way: it provided the townsfolk who were inspired to do so with any number of ways to end their adventures and move on to the world of the dead. It was only then that he noticed the kitchen was as cold as a morgue. Nobody had lit the fire, though that was not why it was so cold. The window was half-open and banging. Finally, he reached the table and picked up the letter. He held it as if, despite the cold, it was on fire.

Outside it was snowing hard again. Gusts of wind shook the windowpanes. From upstairs he could hear Cesare Calò yelling blue murder at little Danilo, who had been up to some mischief, though even the deaf would be able to tell it was more like a nervous rant caused by some inner turmoil. Apart from that, the only sound was coming from the hissing of a log that was a little too green in the fire René had lit. He muttered through his teeth, "Crazy lady. You've broken the eggs for both of us now."

The only good news was that nobody was dead in that empty apartment. René pictured Anna in the woods, wrapped in her warmest clothes, having joined the partisan unit that was fighting through the snowstorm. Anna had left everything behind for a greater calling.

There'd be nothing to be surprised at if he looked in the mirror. His friend had spelt out to him what she'd been planning on doing. Since Edoardo's death, she'd talked about nothing else. René had been as stubborn as a mule. Well, now he could admit it: he'd never believed her. He had never thought she would actually be willing to throw herself into the Resistance like that. They were just things she had said for the sake of it, to let off steam for a few minutes. Or so he'd thought. And now, just look. She had done it. How was she right now? Who was she talking to? About what? Was she cold?

He went over to the fireplace. He pulled the letter out of his pocket. He was tempted to read it one last time, but then decided against it. Without much conviction, he threw it onto the log. The sheet fell ink-side down. A moment later, it caught fire. He watched the paper curl and flutter up the chimney in fragments.

Dear friend . . . her voice continued to ring inside his head. There was no way to silence it. Aside from everything else, he felt betrayed.

He closed the shutters and got ready for bed. That was his usual way of dealing with storms. Whether they were raging inside him or outdoors, it made no difference; he would simply hunker down under the covers. But this time, it was not enough. In fact, the dark and the immobility were eating him alive. He closed his eyes and passages from Anna's letter flashed in front of him, silhouetted against the night. René tossed and turned on the bed, writhing like a snake.

He could always ignore the madwoman's request, of course, but it would be cold-hearted of him. He would never be able to look at his reflection in a store window again. Then he told himself that, all things considered, she hadn't asked him to paint the sky a different color. The mission could be simply stated: Settebello was to carry on being Settebello. He was to go out at the same time as usual and devote his days to acting normal. The only difference was that he was to keep up the appearance that his old friend, who had anyway been hiding herself away all this time, was still living in her apartment.

He was to pretend to do a little shopping for her, as he had always done. To spend a minute of his precious time opening her shutters so that people would think she was home as usual: a task anyone could have done with their eyes closed, even young Calò. That was the purpose of the cookie tin: it contained the little she had saved, so as not to burden the finances of a humble cobbler. Using the secret key, he thought it would be a good move to continue his brief evening visits.

In short, he was to cover for her. Pretend she was in one place, when she was actually occupied somewhere else. None of it required bending over backwards. And anyway, it was a form of protection. Anna would be able to come home at any time without raising any suspicions. An ace up his sleeve if he ever needed it.

The bells were ringing at midnight. He counted the chimes, but sleep eluded him. In the meantime, the storm shook the door hinges and drafts howled around the house.

Anna was out there, in the company of who knows who. René went so far as to wonder whether she had fallen in love with one of them. That may have been his worst moment. He felt used. Worse, he felt that the contrary wind he had been struggling against for the last few years had swept away the only person he had left. A friend? An impossible love? It didn't matter: the band of partisans had stolen her from him. He began to fantasize about no longer sitting on the sidelines, about raiding his wardrobe, throwing on everything he owned, and vanishing into the woods. But he was so tired.

5

M aking the most of the deadly calm in the hallway, he let himself into Anna's house to open the blinds. It may have seemed an easy thing, but opening shutters right onto a street meant exercising extreme caution. In Le Case, windows were like a thousand eyes. Doing something that obvious first thing in the morning would be hard for Settebello to hide. There would be a scandal, to boot. "The Rambaldi widow has found a companion for the night . . . " The man everyone had always seen as a brother to her, almost an uncle to the boy who had recently faced a firing squad. After checking that nothing was going on in the street or in the building opposite, he sprang into action like a spider catching a fly to drag back to its web, certain he had not been seen from any angle.

If someone had told him a week ago that on December 11, he would be having heart palpitations of this magnitude, he wouldn't have believed them. And yet, there he was walking his usual route with a spring in his step that surprised even him. He was bidding everyone good morning in unnaturally high spirits, yet still managing to look nervous. He realized just in time and hastened his pace. It would be a fatal mistake if people were to register that Settebello's mood had changed. When he got to the workshop, he yanked open the door as if he were in a rush for the bathroom. It was only after he had closed it behind him that he understood he needed to calm down.

"What the hell are you doing?" An occasional flash of insight would bring him back to earth. Fully intending to get himself out of Anna's cock-eyed scheme, he answered his own question. "I'm not doing anything." And it was true. Apart from letting a little light into Anna's apartment, he was guilty of no other crime. Yet, scarier thoughts crowded in. What if Anna were arrested and ended up talking? Or any of the other partisans? "There's a man in Via Roma covering for a revolutionary." Anyone would give him up after taking a pummeling. For a moment he had to fight the temptation to run to Rizziello and report the kidnapping of an upstanding citizen. For all he knew, it might even have been true.

When the workshop door opened, he nearly jumped out of his skin, as if he'd been caught red-handed. Mandela chuckled. "René, you've gone pale. Is my mug really that ugly?"

René's heart was still in his throat. "Oh, Claudio. Ciao. Sorry, I was miles away . . . "

Claudio looked around with the habitual sneer of disgust he levelled at everyone and everything. In Le Case, people would count their syllables if they were forced to have dealings with him. It was no secret that he had been fanatical about setting up the garrison. His entire purpose in life appeared to be to win a medal. "And what were you thinking about?" he asked.

René shrugged. "What everyone thinks about . . . " He realized too late that he had just provided the kind of answer that people like Claudio Montalti go to town on. Having failed to make the grade, he strutted around as if he were a colonel. He took a step closer and asked inquisitively, "And what is everyone thinking about?

"That an unforgettable winter is on its way, my friend. Not at all in a good way. Rations are woefully low; families are suffering. I'm thinking that anyone who can, should lend a hand. If not now, when?"

Mandela nodded vaguely, then cleared his throat. "This moment requires sacrifice." That was just the kind of phrase he would spout, as if he were an emanation of the ministry. "The government is working day and night. We need to be patient."

There was a pause. As always when you talked to Claudio Montalti, the conversation would run aground, especially if topics like this came up. Then René saw he was holding a bag. "Did you bring me something?"

This time, it was Mandela who'd been roused from a reverie. "Yes," he said, marching over to the counter in two strides. He laid the package out. "Speaking of lending a hand, my wife's dress is suddenly too wide on the hips. War is war, but you know what women are like. The pins are already in place. Do you think Anna can take it in?"

René took longer than necessary to answer, as if he had been pinned down himself. Montalti brought him back to order. "Hey there, did someone cast a spell?"

"Of course, I'd be happy to take it to her." He blamed his insomnia: at a certain age it can happen. He could only get to sleep after half a flask, but the following day was a nightmare. He'd been feeling under the weather for days.

"Salt," Mandela said.

"What did you say?"

"Before going out, put half a teaspoon of salt under your tongue. It's good for your concentration."

Now he was taking Dr. Salghini's place.

"Thanks for the tip."

"Listen, what can you tell me about her?"

"Her who?"

The retort must have sounded hollow. Everyone knew Settebello's circumstances, and there was no way Claudio Montalti meant a wife, a daughter, or a niece. "Anna," he said in a serious voice. "How is she doing?"

René wanted to put some distance between them and run a mile. Instead, he started gathering his tools together as if he needed to get back to work. "How do you think she's doing?

All she talks about is Edoardo. Maybe she hasn't accepted what has happened yet. After all, she's a mother. Wounds like that never heal."

Mandela looked genuinely shocked. For a moment, René thought the cop act was a disguise that didn't really suit him. His visitor said, "If it had happened to me, I would have shot myself."

René thought of Giovanni, Montalti Jr., whom they called Beccofino because of his thin nose. As far as he knew, the boy had moved up north. He felt obliged to ask after him but the other man had been faster to the draw. He sighed deeply and shook his head. "A partisan for a son. Can you imagine?"

For a moment, a picture of Edoardo at six or seven, intent on making a catapult right there where this well-dressed customer was now standing, flashed through his mind. Mandela went on, "Well, in my case, I would ask myself one question: 'What did I do wrong?' Then I would throw myself off the cliff at Sassoforte."

There was that silence again, which Montalti broke after a while. "I hope keeping herself busy taking in this dress gives Anna a little comfort." He touched his hat. "René, I'll see you tomorrow." Having said this, he went to the door. Before closing it, he added, as usual, "I trust you'll do your duty." Mandela loved using this expression when taking his leave, carabiniere style.

"Of course," René answered.

6

René realized that if Mandela had come by two days earlier, Anna would now be busy taking in the lovely Loredana's dress and would most likely have delayed her caper. She may even have changed her mind about the whole mad plan she had been about to set into action. It was quite normal for the townsfolk to bring him little jobs for Anna to do. After Edoardo had been executed at Gabellino, in fact, people had stopped knocking on her door at 66, Via Roma. A strange aura had descended over the apartment, and she had practically become a recluse there.

The only danger for René was little Danilo: bored all day at home, he often decided to go and play in the stairwell. With the child around, it was impossible to sneak downstairs. Luckily, the boy's breaks were never very long. Rosa's voice would soon echo down the stairs calling him back to sit by the fire. Rapid little steps and a thud of the door were René's green light.

He couldn't count the number of afternoons he had spent in that apartment, with Anna bent over her sewing by the window. He knew where she kept her materials and being a cobbler gave him an advantage: leather or cloth, it was still sewing.

He set to work altering Loredana Montalti's dress. He did a good job. The point was to do justice to Anna's work and replicate a woman's touch. Their client must never be in a position to complain about a single stitch. René was so absorbed by the task that when the church bell chimed three, he was still at the table. He jumped to his feet.

*

He saw a soldier holding a sack standing in front of the workshop. He was stamping his feet to keep them warm and, as soon as he saw the cobbler, he let loose, "Come, you son of a bitch."

There was nothing of the carefree young man he had met a few days before. The few words he said were unnatural and overwrought. But he had brought a good cache from the seminary. There were three pairs of boots to mend—standing around in them all day with wet feet in the snow had reduced the soldiers to tears. Two of them were out of commission with chilblains. The job was urgent: everything had to be ready the following morning, without question. René took the delivery slip and watched the soldier leave without saying goodbye.

It wasn't a huge job in itself, but he would have to eke out his materials. In any case, there was a long shift ahead of him and he needed to work at breakneck speed.

He worked nimbly, though his hands were so cold he had to slap them against his coat to get any sensation in them. Called to order with a clear-cut task, Anna's adventures were pushed back into a sphere of delirium. Had he really thought he could lend himself to such an outlandish request? Well, the answer was yes. Loredana's dress, wrapped and ready to be picked up, was proof. It was the stuff of madness.

When he left the workshop, he saw that the town had been blessed with a magical night. The sky was so clear it was almost frightening, with ice statues made of piled-up snow everywhere. The eerie silence and dark windows made him feel like the last person on earth. The chill knifed through him, but he took his time anyway. His building was already in sight when a patrol van turned into the end of the road.

He instinctively flattened himself against the wall, though he had nothing to fear. If anyone asked him what he was doing out so late, in violation of the curfew, he had a ready answer: he had been mending the boots those very soldiers would be wearing tomorrow. He was working for the seminary; they could check if they wanted. But he didn't want to be in the soldiers' sights. His gaze fell on Anna's ground-floor apartment.

He cursed Mandela several times over. It was all his fault. In order to finish his wife's dress, he had been so late he'd then been forced to rush to get the workshop open without raising any suspicion. Being in such a hurry, he hadn't closed the shutters or turned the lights off in the corridor. Hers was the only window in the whole town that was still lit up. The patrol was sure to notice.

He walked the last stretch risking a nasty slip and almost fell against the front door. He was so nervous that the thud echoed around the street. He watched the van creeping slowly towards him. He went inside, grabbed the secret key, and let himself in right away. The first thing he did was turn the light off. Then he rushed to the sitting room.

He decided to throw all his chips on the table at once: he opened the windows wide and pulled the shutters towards him, careful not to bang them. He stood there listening, his heart thumping.

Through the slats, he could see the van drive slowly down the street on the packed ice. There were three, maybe four, young soldiers inside. They didn't even look up. They lowered a window and a puff of white smoke wafted into the night. They tossed the butt out. René only closed the window once the sound of the engine had faded past the widening in the road near the butcher's.

He stood there in the dark, silent room. Then he groped his way over to the old armchair he knew was nearby. It felt like a swarm of insects was crawling through his bloodstream. He stretched his legs out and caught his breath. "Look what you're making me do," he muttered to Anna, then he started chuckling to himself like a fool. He realized he had probably lost his mind already because something suddenly happened in the emptiness of the apartment: a ghost was blowing an inexplicable sense of wellbeing into his mouth. René sat still so as not to break the spell. He closed his eyes for a second.

A horn sounded from the road. Looking around, he had no idea where he was. Had he been arrested and locked up somewhere? He soon realized what had happened: his bones weren't aching because he'd been beaten; that skeleton of an armchair where he had spent the night soaking up all the ice in Maremma was to blame.

It was hard enough to get up, but it was his neck that made him see stars. That's how you end up when you're past fifty and you nod off for hours with your chin on your chest. He realized he was hungry. He hadn't touched any food since lunch the day before, and that hadn't exactly been a feast.

The needles, thread, and cut-offs from Loredana Montalti's dress were still on the table. But there was almost nothing in the kitchen cupboard. That fact alone was enough to kill his appetite: she had clearly planned her escape well.

All of a sudden, he was overwhelmed by questions he had often asked himself. What did the partisans want? Why were they doing it? How did they come to believe in their cause? What were the chances that they were just a bunch of Godless oddballs?

He would often think about these issues and he felt like a poor idiot who had been unable to see the light when it came to certain things. He had always kowtowed to authority, constantly saying "Yes, Sir. No, Sir!" even when it made him spit bile. Those young men in the woods were not like that. Anna had opened her eyes, though for her it was different: she had joined the revolution out of revenge. And that was more than enough. Was there anything worse than killing a woman's son? Shouldering a rifle was the least she could do. But the others?

What motivated them? They never gave up, which made matters worse. They didn't care that they were scared or hungry or even that they might die. Deserters had been discovered among their ranks and the partisans would sooner have allowed their families to be exterminated than give up their fellow fighters. What secret made them do such terrible things?

Edoardo. When René closed his eyes, he would see him in a series of flashes at every possible age: in his workshop, in town, at home. Once, when they had been talking about the boy carrying a torch for pretty Sveva Pacchetti, Anna had commented, "We brought him up well." She had said "we." Then the boy joined the partisans. They thought he had been fighting in the war and then the news came in from Gabellino. René would never have imagined contributing to something like that.

nna says the usual."

Mandela looked at the package, arching his eyebrows as if to say, "Nice way to thank me. Not even a little discount?" But he took his wallet out without saying a word. At that very moment, the workshop door opened.

A man came in. He was wearing a jacket that was so threadbare his whole body was shaking, his shoulders hunched against the cold. The man noticed there was a customer and held back, just inside the door.

You could have cut the atmosphere with a knife, and with good reason: the man was a prisoner from the villa. Mandela stared and jutted his chin forward. He quickly took charge of the situation. "Well? Have you lost your way home?"

The man lowered his head and started searching through his pockets. He pulled out a slip of paper. "I'm here to pick up an order," he said quietly, attempting to show the cobbler the order form for the boots.

"One moment," René said, turning back to Montalti and handing him the package. "Please send my regards to Loredana."

But Mandela had sniffed out an opportunity for entertainment. "Of course. Business at the villa takes precedence," he said, stepping aside. He bowed to the prisoner, "At your service."

René decided to take his time and give the poor man, who was shuddering and coughing, a chance to thaw out.

The prisoner shuffled forward and Claudio Montalti stepped back at exactly the same moment, until they were practically touching. Montalti's chest brushed against the prisoner. "Watch your step, my good man." Then, turning to the cobbler, "See how things work around here? They think they own the world. But their days are numbered, right René?"

Settebello bent down behind the counter without answering and picked up the sack filled with boots. The prisoner took it. His knuckles were white, rubbed raw by the north wind. He dropped the slip by the cash register. "They'll come and pay," he mumbled almost inaudibly as he made his way back to the door.

"Just one question," Mandela interrupted. "René, I paid up what I owed you, didn't I?"

The only good thing about the prevarication was that the more they talked, the longer the poor man could stay in the warm. "Yes, Claudio. You did."

Montalti gave a satisfied nod. "Meaning that when someone receives a service, it's good practice to pay the person who has provided that service right away. Am I wrong?"

"We have agreements with the villa that—"

"René, have you noticed? Whenever these lowlifes are around, this is what happens: they pick up the consignment and leave. As if they were owed everything."

The man listened in silence, staring at the door. "I don't have permission to handle money," he said finally. "The person in charge will be back and will pay the cobbler what was agreed. Good day to you."

Mandela made a clown's face, as if he couldn't believe his ears. "René, did you hear that? Our friend here says Jews aren't allowed to handle money. No, that is too much. Does he mean that the world is changing direction? Good man, are they treating you alright?"

"They give us everything we need."

"René, do you hear him? These people are like woodpeckers. In the warm, fattening up. No work, some of them cook. They even have their personal cobbler. There's no better time to be one of their ilk! And here we are suffering day after day. When all's said and done, they are right." He looked at the prisoner from head to toe. "Where do you come from?"

"Arcidosso."

"Get that! I had a cousin there once. We may turn out to be half-related." He turned serious. He leaned towards the prisoner's ear as if his nose were approaching a pile of shit. "Don't get your hopes up. In our family we have a bit of everything, from madmen to brigands. We even had an uncle from Campagnatico who was basically a faggot. But we don't have animals in the family. Of that, I'm sure."

A blond soldier tapped the butt of his rifle twice on the glass in the door. Mandela practically leaped to attention and made as if to salute. He was totally ignored. The soldier called from outside, pointing at the prisoner. "Move!" The prisoner set off, "Have a good day."

The silence he left in his wake was not the usual pause that followed Claudio Montalti's having run a conversation into the ground. He seemed to be suffering because René hadn't indulged him in any way. The workshop felt like it was shrinking around them. Finally, he could stand it no longer. He picked up the package for his wife and said, "Send my regards to Anna." Then, he left without looking back. And without the stupid carabiniere warning.

8

In other circumstances, he might have set himself up in the bar, but he had to be in the right mood to set foot in the Due Porte. He wasn't always ready to play along with the endless Settebello cracks. Nevertheless, it was the only place where he could get wind of the rumors that were flying around; despite the shortages, nobody begrudged themselves a drop of liquor before lunch to stave off the hunger pangs. The soldiers were not keen on gatherings and they sometimes came in armed to the hilt to round people up. If there were too many men propping up Maso's bar, some of them might get kicked out to give the place an appearance of propriety. That was why different neighborhoods took turns, waiting for the clock to strike before setting out for a quick drink.

When they saw him arrive, nobody bothered to greet him. The three men René found there instinctively shot a glance around the room, gauging whether they would be kicked out and sent home. He waited at the door for a nod from Maso, who pretended everything was normal and called out, "Hey, Settebello. We haven't seen you in here for a while."

René asked for an espresso and a glass of strong red wine.

He didn't need to be a rocket scientist to see that the mood at Due Porte was more somber than ever. The three men at the counter looked cataleptic. Zoni was the worst: his face was bright red and his eyes like dark little beads. The place was so bleak it didn't even feel like a bar. They were talking in the hushed tones they used in Dr. Salghini's waiting room. Maso placed the coffee in front of him and went to get the wine. "So, what's up?" He wanted to chat. It can't be fun watching the same rerun every night—the townsfolk drowning their troubles in his bar.

René shrugged. "Business is so bad it would put a saint to sleep; best not talk about it. What about you? What's going on?"

"Holy moly," Colica called over from the table in the back. But Maso cut him short. "Giancarlo, please! Any more cussing and I'll toss you out of here with a pitchfork."

The exchange made everyone chuckle. Pious Maso's ongoing crusade against certain characters in town was a classic. Behind the bar of Le Case was this charismatic man who fought a daily battle against the poisoned blood that caused people to blaspheme Jesus with every greeting, war or no war.

"Same old, same old," Maso said turning to René. "Meaning worse than ever. First Mattafirri comes in, barking like a rabid dog saying, 'I've got money and there's nothing to buy!' The rations are a piss in the pot. If anyone had said it would come to this, I would never have believed them back then. Look at me: these poor bastards are turning bread into wine, and a few pennies land in the cash register, but what am I supposed to do with the money?"

René drank his espresso in one gulp. "Same here. You know, they've started bringing in boots from the villa. I'm not complaining. The rates are decent enough, but it's just loose change. I ring it through the till and that's the end of it."

He hadn't meant to mention the bishop's villa. René picked up the glass of wine as if he'd forgotten about it. He had just taken his first sip when Corrado Nencioni butted in: "That place was just what we needed."

"Pig of a—."

"Giancarlo!" Maso yelled.

Colica responded with a burp.

"They say they've started to give themselves up," Nencioni

went on, lowering his voice. "They arrive on the bus or in their chauffeur-driven cars loaded up with luggage. Then they knock on the door of the garrison and sign themselves in for the prison camp."

"They're as sly as foxes," Zoni commented.

Corrado winked at his buddy. "The thing is, word has gotten around. The camp at the villa may be surrounded by barbed wire but, at the end of the day, they're treated well. If you were in their position, and someone told you there was a safe place close to home, what would you do? The alternative is to wait for the soldiers to come at night and carry you off God knows where in your underpants. They say families are kept together at the villa."

Evaristo Zoni stared into space. "How should I know?"

It was Tiziano Battistini's turn. His nickname was Farfallina, after his fall from the top of San Martino when he was ten made him the stuff of legend. Anyone else would have been splattered everywhere, but the only consequence for him was a limp. He had been too light to gain any velocity and flew like a little butterfly, everyone had said "I still can't fathom it," he said. "A prison camp at Le Case. It must mean something or other."

Zoni answered without even turning around: "Ugliness leads to more ugliness. They're not going to come and build a dance hall up here, are they?"

"On church land, to boot," Nencioni continued, looking genuinely shocked. "I still can't believe it."

"Everything is by design," Maso murmured. Four words that gained traction.

Farfallina rapped his knuckles on the table. "Let's not get started with your priest's fancies. I've never cared a fig for the seminary, but turning it into a prison and locking people up there is unacceptable. They're doing it right here under our noses, as if they know what kind of people we are. Sure that nobody will lift a finger. I don't want the burden of guilt. I swear I can't sleep at night. If only I were twenty years younger . . . "

"You'd still be a cripple," Colica chuckled.

Battistini looked at Colica with loathing. "That's exactly what I mean. This ugliness. Everything is a joke, a stupid laugh. All that matters is being here, guzzling our drinks and clutching our balls while the world outside is veering off in a different direction."

It didn't look like the words upset Giancarlo Franci. "Well, go on then. Go and get yourself shot and you'll be done with it."

Farfallina looked as though the air had been punched out of him. He attempted a smile, but his face was a death mask. "Do you know what I think? A prison camp on the outskirts of our town is exactly what we deserve." The conversation should have ended there, but he was angry and he couldn't keep his mouth shut. "If I were twenty years younger, I would have joined the partisans in the woods long ago."

These words brought them all back to square one. At the Due Porte people acted as if they were friends, but these days, things were fraught: any one of them could be a spy for the Maresciallo. Things were so bad that a few bills were enough to persuade someone to blabber.

Keen to avoid a brawl in his bar, Maso reined in the conversation. "Listen, the next round is on me. Who wants a drink?"

But the damage had already been done. Their faces had sunk deeper than hell. Farfallina grabbed his stick and managed to pull himself up onto his feet with a few jerky movements. "I came here to find comfort and I'm going home sicker than ever," he muttered to himself.

They watched him shuffle out. Not one of those noble souls thought to say something like, "Come on, let's not take it out on one another here . . . " Not Maso. Not even René. There was one simple reason and it had made them clam up like kids caught with their fingers in the pie: Farfallina had been right.

9

He woke up from his afternoon nap with Battistini's words still in his ears. A quick glance out of the window, and he made up his mind: it was one of those days when it would be best to stay home and not go to the workshop. With a snow storm of that magnitude, it would be foolish to venture out unless it was necessary. A thought flickered through his body, warming him up on the spot. "I'll go down to Anna's and we'll spend a little time together." But the flame died out immediately: she was in the woods. Downstairs, there was nothing but empty rooms.

René still couldn't get his head around it. All she'd had to say was, "I've made up my mind." No conjectures or explanations; just facts. Anna knew perfectly well that he would never give her secret away. She'd had years to test him out and had finally decided he wasn't on her team. That's when she had jumped ship. What had he stayed back here to do? Sit in front of the dying embers huddled up in an old blanket that reeked of old blanket? His only task was to keep the ghost of his friend alive, while she lay in someone else's arms, somewhere in a partisan cave.

The bells of St. Bastian's chimed two. Outside, the weather was worsening: the white-out was so complete, you couldn't see the street. The building opposite might well have never existed. René said out loud: "Shall I go or not?"

As he opened his front door, he gripped the handle tight, jiggling it as to avoid even the slightest creak. The stairwell was empty; no sign of little Calò. He slipped out as stealthily as a cat and tiptoed down the stairs.

The lights in the hall were like the remembrance candles in the cemetery chapel built by the Isastias; everyone would stop for a peek when they went to tend their loved one's graves. He bent down to get the hidden key and unlocked the door. He closed the door behind him quietly. Then everything went blank.

The first thing he heard was, "We need to move . . . "

Then, sounding like a breath of wind, "First, we need to wake him up."

Another voice, "Faina, have you got everything?"

The first voice again, "I think so. Will you hurry up?"

The voices were just like the ones in the dream he'd been having about Farfallina, only more real.

"His eyes are open."

Someone else said, "If the storm dies down, we'll be sitting ducks."

"Who are you?" René asked, attempting to pull himself up. His head span and he fell back down, staring at the ceiling.

He saw a face appear above him, "Calm down."

He was so thrown that the name came out spontaneously. "Edoardo?" The shadow looked just like him.

Another, louder voice. "Hey, can you hear me?" a man said, grabbing René's chin and shaking it.

"You'll make him vomit."

"Who are you?" he tried again. It was only then that he remembered that Edoardo's beard had a reddish hue to it. But he couldn't fathom any of it. The man stank of cigarettes. He said, "Are you René?"

The giant next to him answered, "Who do you think he is? Look at his hand."

"It's me," the cobbler answered, as if he were speaking in

a dream. He tried again to pull himself up onto one elbow. A strange ringing started in his right ear. "What did you do to me?"

From somewhere else in the room came more words: "I'm not saying it again. We need to get going."

"Let's wake him up properly first," the big man said. "If he starts yelling, he'll burn our safehouse."

Edoardo was not Edoardo at all: he had the beaked nose of a falcon and round misted-up glasses. He said, "Faina, this is all your fault. Just be patient."

Some fast steps, and another shadow entered his field of vision. "What was I supposed to do? I saw the door being opened. As far as I knew, it could have been Ercolani in person."

Surprisingly, the giant had the face of an overgrown child, with a wispy moustache. "You need to calm down," he said, turning to his comrade. "Before using your hands, count to three. Anna warned us that . . . "

"Anna?" René said, with a start. Hearing her name was better than a hundred slaps to bring him back to earth. "Where is she?"

"She's well," the man in glasses said.

That was not enough. "Where is she?"

Finally, René managed to haul himself almost into a sitting position. The two men leaned down and helped, grabbing him and then heaving him up until his back was against the wall.

They were in the corridor, close to the door. René could see them more clearly: they were wearing heavy jackets and hats. The big man had a cape with a hood. The eldest couldn't have been more than twenty-five. Three rifles were leaning against the kitchen hatch.

"Are you feeling better?" the skinny one he had mistaken for Edoardo asked.

René didn't know how he was, he wasn't even sure he had woken up from his nap. There was a pulsing in his temple above his right ear, which was buzzing. He touched it and saw there was blood on his hand.

The man in the middle came forward. "Come on. What's with all the fuss? I didn't hit you that hard."

"It was a wallop, and you can see what you did," the overgrown boy stated.

The other man huffed, unhappy with the criticism. "Let's go."

"How did you get in?"

The bespectacled partisan crouched down. He had assigned himself the task of calming down their chance visitor. "We have the keys," he said. "Under cover of the snow storm, we came down to the road from the mountain. It was hard to see which building was hers."

René had only one concern: "Where is Anna?"

The man who had hit him started to pace up and down. "Don't you have any other questions?" He gave his companion a little kick. "Mosca, I'm telling you; we need to get going."

The man in glasses didn't move. "She's fine," he said, looking the cobbler straight in the eye. "She's already chosen her battle name—Ombra, shadow. Remember it; it's important."

The words caught in René's throat. He blinked away the tears that were making him see double. "And . . . " he started, unsure how to go on.

"She had a great idea: a hideout in the middle of town. And you are working for all of us here. Actually, you are on the front line, working for the cause. Speaking of which, thank you for what you are doing. It's very important to us."

The giant let out a huff. "Thanking strongman Maciste here with a blow to the head wasn't exactly a brilliant move."

"Maciste?" René said.

Mosca smiled. "That's what we call you."

He looked at the group of men, bewildered. "You've given me a battle name, too?"

"She chose it for you."

The idea made him feel giddy, and it had nothing to do with the blow. From Pistola to Settebello to Maciste. Just thinking about it made different parts of him fit together differently. "What were you doing here?"

The partisan they called Faina, who was clearly as shrewd as the ferret he'd chosen as his namesake, glanced out of the window. "Listen, the storm is still raging, but . . . "

His comrade ignored him. "We have a wounded man here. A bad fall. We need something to clean and patch up the wound before it gets infected."

René's mind went to the needles and thread. "Well, over there are some . . . "

"We know. Ombra was very clear."

"Is she ever coming back?"

Mosca studied him for a while without answering. Then his expression changed. "It may be a bit too soon to talk to you about it, but since we're all here . . . "

Faina let out a deep sigh. "Get on with it, though."

"We have a plan," the partisan in glasses murmured.

"What plan? And why do you need to talk to me about it?"

The young man looked as though he was searching for the right words. In the end, he chose two. "The villa."

"You mean . . . ?"

"There are some prisoners who communicate with our moles almost every day. We have a couple of highly trusted ones in Le Case. The soldiers are pretty lax when they take prisoners on their errands, and we've taken advantage of it. Some of them go into stores and . . . basically, that is where messages are exchanged."

René thought about how relieved Farfallina would be to hear this unexpected news: not everyone in town was a drunken egotist; some people were resisting quietly. "What do they tell you?"

"For now, we're gathering information about how the camp works, how it was set up, what kind of equipment the soldiers have, the guard-duty shifts . . . "

He was reminded of Anna on her birthday, full of talk about sentry towers and machine guns. He asked them straight out. "Are you planning an attack?"

Mosca turned serious. "We'll see about that. Certainly, getting access to their weapons deposit would be a coup. In any case, we can't leave those families there. There are children. And a pregnant woman."

The ringing in his ears grew shriller. His heart, too, had started beating differently. "Why are you telling me all this?"

The person who spoke up was the colossus in a cape. "They know who you are."

"They . . . ?" René asked in the tone of someone who knew he was doomed.

Mosca smiled. "We've been keeping an eye on you."

He thought of the prisoner Mandela had provoked. As soon as he'd returned to the camp, he'd probably told his companions about his adventure at the cobbler's. Then he thought back to the discussion at the Due Porte: could there have been a partisan mole in there amongst all the usual faces? What else had he missed since Anna had vanished? His voice had already steadied by the time he asked: "What am I supposed to do?"

Faina retorted, "For heaven's sake, absolutely nothing."

"Exactly," Mosca confirmed, as if he were relaying orders from Moscow central. "You stay here, carry on with your life at the workshop and your daily checks on your friend." He paused, as if to make sure René hadn't missed a word. Then he added, "When the time comes, we'll be in touch."

10.

Christmas seemed to have been erased from the calendar. The freeze wouldn't loosen its grip and rations were so low that families were going to bed with stones in their stomachs. The Calò family was no exception; little Danilo had caught a chest infection and had been out of action for at least a week. Rosa was worried sick, quickly turning into the ghost of her beautiful, sunny self. Her husband did odd jobs in the houses of the elderly with no families, and received packets of salt or potatoes as payment. The icy nights clearly meant that this was just the beginning. There was no choice for anyone but to stay put and cover up, as if they were taking refuge from a scavenging animal. Nobody was in the mood to celebrate the birth of baby Jesus.

When René saw the rope team of miserable waifs shuffle past, he went to the door of his workshop. The trips had turned into torture: the soldiers would spin the excursions out so that they could stay in the warm as long as possible, and the prisoners would be left to freeze in front of St. Bastian's, wearing the same clothes they had arrived in. René spotted the internee who had brought him the boots and wondered again whether he was one of the partisan informers on the inside. Did the inmate know who René was? If he had not bumped into Mandela that day, would he have tried to communicate with him? Whatever the case, they were good at what they were doing. Sticking to the side of the road, not one of them turned to peer at the cobbler. Also, there had been no sign of the women prisoners.

At the Due Porte, the same old story was being bandied about: the prisoners were being treated well. Some would fly into a rant, cursing the Jews and claiming that, if only they had been born Jewish, they would now be warm and comfortable, rather than out foraging for food for their children, who were beginning to look more and more like skinned hares. Anyone mouthing off would soon be put to shame and made to feel like a chicken thief. They had all heard horrific stories about these people on BBC Radio Londra. People weren't thinking straight because they were scared.

The news from Ortona was not commented on, since celebrating the Allies' advancing army was dangerous. But help no longer felt so far away. And yet, up where they were in the mountains, there seemed to be a different set of rules. Rumor had it that a certain well-connected prisoner would occasionally pay a visit to the Maresciallo's house, where they would sit down together—one a Jew and the other a Fascist—and listen to news from the front. Stories like these would stir up the more troubled souls. Any form of favoritism based on money or connections drove them off the edge. The upshot was that the Maremma-born-and-bred Jews imprisoned behind barbed wire had been turned into enemies. Knowing they had been interned was bad, but imagining them getting benefits while ordinary people were slowly dying was too much.

Le Case was like a wild animal rearing to pick a fight. René could only start breathing freely when he let himself into Anna's apartment. He never did much: he would maybe spend an hour or so in the kitchen looking out of the window at the woods, or clean things up, taking care not to poke his nose into things that weren't any of his business. Every now and again, he would say his battle name to himself. It was like putting on an extra layer of skin that was beginning to feel like his own. Who would have thought that one day he would have the secret nickname of a muscle-man like Maciste? It was the only thing that kept him company.

Dr. Salghini came into the workshop just as René was wrapping up to leave. "Good evening," he said, slapping his thighs. He had nothing with him, not even his doctor's bag.

"Emilio, still out at this hour?"

The local doctor went straight to the stove, where a single log was half-buried in a pile of ash. "I'll stop for a minute then send the day to hell in a handcart, like you."

"Warm up. We're our own bosses."

The doctor nodded, shaking all over. Then he said, "Can you believe it? According to the calendar, the first day of winter was the day before yesterday. It feels like it's been winter since the day I was born."

"It'll come to an end. It always does."

"Getting through it this year is going to be a challenge. That's why I'm here."

"Because it's winter?"

Salghini shook his head. "Families are on their knees and the rations are running out. The old and the very young are getting weaker. In the more fortunate cases, they end up in bed with phlegm in their chests. I do everything in my power to give them courage, but who is going to give me the strength to go on?"

"The Calò kid has been ill, too, but it looks like he's on the mend."

"How are you feeling?"

"Me? Thank God, I keep going. I shouldn't say it, or I might bring bad luck onto myself."

"Good for you. I've started going around the different neighborhoods to gauge for myself how bad it's going to be. It's not just bread that's scarce; I'm running low on medicines. That's without taking into account this situation at the villa: between prisoners and soldiers, there must be at least a hundred more mouths to feed than normal. Crowd that many extra people who all have to eat and shit into one town, and things will go to hell in no time. Ercolani hasn't thought this one through: he's willing to put the whole town through the wringer so he can look good with the Fascists. And, as I was saying, winter has just arrived. It won't be easy to get supplies. In short, there's a disaster on the way."

They sat there for a while, overcome with gloom. Then Salghini clapped his hands, as if he were trying to give himself some energy. "So, what can you tell me about Anna? I don't know whether I'll manage to go by her place tomorrow, but by Christmas Day, I hope to have visited the whole of Via Roma."

"Anna is fine."

The doctor paused, a little distracted. "You know, thinking about it, I can't remember the last time I saw her."

René was a block of marble. "Edoardo's death was a terrible blow. She doesn't go out if she can avoid it. In this weather . . . "

"I know. Maybe I'll take her some of my special drops, to calm her nerves."

"I really don't think you need to. I stop by every day. Keep your energy for people who actually need your attention."

"Like the Calò family you mentioned. Thanks for reminding me about little Danilo. Knocking at Anna's door is no effort at all. Maybe seeing an old face will distract her for a few minutes."

Yes, well, anyway . . . "

"Now that's enough talk about illness and calamity. All I want is to get home and sit in front of the fire with Vilma. I don't know how she gets through the day all on her own, poor thing. These days, when she sees me coming, her eyes light up. She hadn't looked at me that way for at least twenty years."

Dr. Salghini buttoned up his coat and pulled the lapels up over his ears. "Bye, René," he said. "And don't you dare catch even half of a cold. People don't think of it, but if the cobbler catches his death, we'll all be walking around in cardboard shoes."

He went as far as thinking he'd don Anna's dressing gown and pretend to be her, stuck in bed for some reason. Every idea fell through, however, and he began to curse that band of partisans: they could at least have left him a name or a way to contact them.

Leaving the workshop unmanned on Christmas Eve in order to keep an eye on his building would be a mistake; people might notice. For a moment he thought the only way out would be to take Dr. Salghini aside and tell him the truth. With the risk the doctor would call the Maresciallo's dogs on him—who was to say that the doctor's recce around town wasn't an idea cooked up by Rizziello himself in order to test the terrain and see if any of the townsfolk turned out to be subversives?

René had told everyone that he saw Anna every day. He imagined the scene: Dr. Salghini knocking on her door and receiving no answer. Nobody had set eyes on her. In short, it would soon become evident that she had vanished into thin air from one day to the next. There were several people who would vouch they had seen the cobbler doing a spot of shopping for her on top of his own; the Calò family would say they had seen him go into the apartment regularly until the day before.

Sending Dr. Salghini off somewhere on an urgent mission and thereby gaining a bit of time was another possibility: At one point he surprised himself with an ugly thought, "He might even die tonight."

11.

He had waited anxiously for the line of prisoners to arrive, but when they were there, all he really wanted to
do was run a mile. He watched as they broke ranks to
perform their respective errands, although by then there were
only a few supplies to pick up. Most of the seminary stocks
were delivered from the city. The outings were no more than an
excuse for the soldiers to go to the bar or slip into houses where
girls were waiting for them. The prisoners expedited their tasks
in no time at all and then they gathered in front of the church to
die of cold. René left the workshop.

There was no one in the little square, but the windows all
had eyes, as usual. He hugged the wall and went towards the
widening in the road. The slope was steep: one false step on an
icy rock and he would end up more than a hundred feet below.
The prisoners stared at him as he approached. The little eddies
of wind cut across his face; a nose could be lost to frostbite in
half a minute flat. And yet René was on fire. Desire and fear
propelled him forward, past the houses and almost as far as the
church, as reckless as if he had downed a bottle of wine.

Tying shoelaces was child's play, but for Settebello it required
a skillful twist of the wrist. He had plenty of other things to worry
about, but he was still ashamed to be seen engaged in such an in-
timate task. It was unpleasant to be pitied by prisoners who had
been reduced to the status of pack animals. In order to distract
them from his pathetic maneuvers, he said without lifting his
head, "I have an urgent message for the brigade."

There was no answer.

"The woman who joined Boscaglia needs to get back to her apartment immediately. She's in danger of being discovered."

Still no answer.

He was tempted to add, "If they find out she's gone, they'll realize I'm playing them and torture me until I talk," but opted for another strategy. "Make up an excuse to go back to the shops. Do it now, before the guards get back."

He got back onto his feet. Standing up, his head span and he almost passed out, but he carried on walking anyway. A few seconds later, he made his way to the bottom of Via di Mezzo.

Walking up the hill from the square to the arch was no joke; he had to stop and catch his breath every few steps. He clung to the icy rope that had been placed along the wall and looked back at the prisoners; they were still standing there, exactly as he had left them. All of a sudden, he saw one of them detach himself from the group. "Run," Settebello muttered. Then he set his mind to getting up the hill. After a sleepless night and this latest daring move, a drink at Maso's was the least he deserved.

In another age, he had been excited on Christmas Eve, but back then it was a stocking full of tangerines he would be waiting for, not a troop of soldiers breaking down the door and dragging him away by his hair. His heart missed a beat every time he heard a noise outside. A shutter banging was enough to give him a heart attack.

The whole way home, he imagined soldiers in front of his building. He was wound up so tight that, as he turned into Via Roma, he was tempted to hold out his wrists ready to be handcuffed. But there was nobody there. The only explanation for why they hadn't arrested him yet was that Dr. Salghini hadn't gone to check up on Anna that morning.

He spent his lunch break by the window, like Ciuccia.

He could see the decrepit old woman there right now, in the ground-floor window opposite. She had spent her whole life there. And here he was, becoming her reflection. They were keeping vigil over the deserted street like passengers staring at the same view from a derailed train. At one point, he saw a cat slink by, flattened against the wall as if it were being chased by a load of kicks. St. Bastian's struck one. Then two. By the time it rang three, he was on his way back to the workshop for his afternoon shift.

He started toying with Cacciaferri's moccasins. As usual, the front had come unstuck. She had always been pigeon-toed. The way she walked was the spitting image of the way she lived her life: inward-looking and restrained. Leonilde Cacciaferri walked as if she regretted it. She had recently adopted an ash whip as revenge.

René often thought that "stepping into someone's shoes" was no bad thing. In his view, there wasn't much to it. All he had to do was take the soles off a pair of shoes and he could read the owner's whole story. There were those who banged on their heels, those whose tread was leaden, and those who waddled like ducks. Some of the shoes that came in were rank with the stench of carrion. Farfallina's boots were funny: one was chewed up and the other almost new. There were deformed tops and soles worn out by the balls of feet as if their owners had done nothing but run. Or there were invisible arches, where only the toes had left their mark. Perugini had only four toes on her left foot, a fact that smacked of witchcraft. Heels burned to nothing, split tongues. Pay attention to the feet, and faces look different. When the toe of a woman's shoe is worn out there are only two possibilities: either they have spent a great deal of time kneeling at church or they've been up to you know what.

It had become a bad habit of his: before looking someone in the face, he would take a quick peek at their shoes, which told him a completely different story. He would often spy a character trait that had nothing to do with what was on display. This was true even for kids. Needless to say, Mandela's shoes were as shiny as remorse, the extra heel worn on the outside. He couldn't swear on it, but he was willing to bet that the boots of the cuirassier regiment on parade looked like that.

He knew how everyone in le Case walked: the confidence, caution or consideration they put into it. What kind of attrition they created with the ground, and by extension with everything else. He could sometimes catch people out in a lie. For example, he was looking at Dr. Salghini's shoes that minute. The upper shoe was not sufficiently soaked and the sides were only a little wet. Proving that he had not been walking through the snow from house to house. "René, do you know what I mean?"

He was at the workbench holding Cacciaferri's right shoe. "Of course," he said distractedly.

"Her behavior was nothing like what you described: she was running from one room to another, almost flying. Her eyes sparkled like those of a young girl in love. Do you get my drift? It's worrying, you know. There's a nervous breakdown on the way."

Emilio Salghini had been talking about Anna for the past five minutes. René bade his time, as if he were listening to a story. So, she had come back. The message he had sent via the prisoner had somehow been relayed up into the woods.

"René, are you okay?" the doctor asked when he saw that he was still distracted. Daydreaming like this would tip off the doctor if he wasn't careful.

"She has days like that," he muttered. "It sounds like a good sign to me. It means she's reacting, right?"

"I'm not sure. I'm thinking of Saretta Giuliani, how overwrought she had seemed when they came to tell her that her husband had been killed in the mine explosion. She made him his supper as if nothing had happened. When they left, she vanished, leaving the front door ajar. Do you remember the search party? She had tricked everyone by going down to the cellar and hanging herself there."

René had to be careful not to give anything away with that little smile he could feel unfurling beneath his moustache. "There have been times when I thought Anna might be capable of doing something like that. In fact, I've been keeping a close eye on her. But now, after all this time?"

Dr. Salghini shook his head, not convinced at all. "You can never tell how the windmills of a mother's mind will spin after she has been torn apart by such a terrible event. There's nothing I can do about it. No medicine is strong enough for something like that."

He wanted to ask, "How does she look? Is she still beautiful? Has the cold gotten to her?" He could only imagine it. Part of the problem was that he had to control his instinct to push Dr. Salghini out of the workshop and run down the road to knock loudly on her door and ask her to tell him about her adventures.

Emilio sighed deeply. "The good thing is that she is as strong as a bull. The quicksilver in her must be saving her from this icy spell." After a while, he added, "Remember, the more miserable you are, the more likely it is you will fall ill. It's not scientific, but it's the way it goes."

12

He stared at the flickering log and said out loud, "Who do you take me for? It's all very well being your friend, but you've crossed the line here."

Wind began to blow down the chimney. René was reminded of his mother spitting out *ventigini*, as she called them. The billowing meant that someone was talking ill of the family and the only thing that could send the gossips' curses back was a gob of spit in the fire. He spat and watched as the mucus sizzled on the flames.

He kept picturing himself as the sucker who had run down the road, almost slipping on the ice, shouting to himself, "She's back! She's back!"

Not even a note. No thank you in any shape or form. Nothing. His great friend, for whom he was risking his life, hadn't left a single token of gratitude. René would have been happy with a glass of wine on the table, a sign: "To your health." Anna had played out her charade with Dr. Salghini and then slipped away again. Thank you very much. Send me a postcard.

Now the doctor's words felt like daggers. He had gone on and on about how Anna was in great shape. One phrase in particular had gutted him, and he mulled it over in his mind: "Her eyes were sparkling like those of a young girl in love." Good for her. How on earth could a woman be any use out in the woods, with all that mud and ice, or in the caves where the partisans holed up in the evenings? Maybe Anna sat behind a stove, waiting for the happy brigade to return from their raids? "Time for dinner!" They probably piled up on top of one another, making a ball of bodies to keep warm, feel close, and stay alive. It wasn't such a leap of faith to imagine hands moving, mouths seeking comfort after the umpteenth battle raging all day. A buckle opening, a hand creeping into the folds of a greatcoat.

His fantasies took him to the point he was disgusted at himself. Flaying himself alive wouldn't be enough to strip away those thoughts he didn't want to have. They just kept on coming. He didn't even notice them returning. It was a shooting match between him and himself: one René baying at the moon, mortified by her abandoning him, and another, more daring man saying, "What is keeping you here? Why don't you go and join Anna and that band of beggars?" Why didn't he go? When Anna decided to leave without saying anything, she could easily have been whispering in his ear, "I'm waiting for you. You decide."

He was standing in front of his wardrobe, the doors open. He was giving the daring René an audience. As if he were ready for anything, he said, "If you want to go to war, you don't need anything. Except courage."

But what did that René know about the real René? He had never been in any important battles. All of a sudden, the brave René was enjoying prodding the flaky fifty-year-old. It was easy to preach with a fireplace in the other room. The partisans up in the mountains didn't need big talk; they were looking for strong hands and devoted hearts.

Of course, he would have some wonderful tools to contribute to the court of Boscaglia, including the leather that would be enough to protect the feet of every partisan crawling through the undergrowth from there to Bologna.

A workshop in the woods. The idea suddenly came to him and, for a moment, it felt like the reason and the solution to everything. Since he was too old to serve the cause, he would start a new business in the back of a cave. That was where the revolution would take place—there was no way around it, war was fought with feet. There happened to be a great cobbler, armed with an apron. He lived up in the mountains, like Pinocchio's father in the belly of a whale. He carried out his tasks by candlelight, working for the hundreds of young lads up in the woods so that they wouldn't have go to war with broken boots held together with a threadbare cloth laced up to the knee.

When midnight struck, he was still there. "It's Christmas Day," he said to himself. He had emptied his wardrobe and tossed everything on the bed. He started folding everything up as the other René blew increasingly loud raspberries at him. Well, he had been on the cusp of actually doing it.

He climbed under the covers. The one good thing was that he had tested the secret telephone line with the brigade. He thought back to the man who had suddenly detached himself from the group of prisoners. Who knows which shop he chose to send his message from? Maybe he had ventured into old Fulcheris's shack that stank of old cheese? Or was it Onorina who was unexpectedly communicating with those landlocked pirates in the woods? He didn't want to know. Suddenly, it was more fun to imagine that behind every vexed face there could hide a spirit far from the one that ruled the lowlifes of the old town. Knowing the name of that would be a waste. Better to imagine valor in every possible face.

DEAR ANNA

1.

The German occupation made brutes like Mandela gloat, but it soon became clear that everyone would be getting the boot. There was to be no loitering. People could go out to pick up rations or keep stores open for the soldiers. The Due Porte was in that category, but if any of the townsfolk were caught drinking as a dare or just for the hell of it, they were in trouble. Trouble was precisely where Farfallina landed—he was beaten up so badly it almost killed him. They said his face had been caved in and that all it had taken was two strikes with a rifle butt. After the news made the rounds of the town, everyone's face looked just as caved in. In the short distance between Dr. Salghini's clinic and Don Lauro's rectory anyone who ventured out could be lined up against the wall and shot. Standing at the window singing, the Calò boy had found himself looking at a machine gun aimed at him from the street.

The prisoners were no longer brought into town. This meant no more contact with Mosca, Faina, or Boscaglia. Just by opening and closing Anna's shutters René risked arrest and a painful death in a cell.

The townsfolk used their eyes to give one another courage. There was nothing else they could do without running the risk of chancing upon a couple of disgruntled Nazis, who answered to no one and who would fondle a woman right in front of her husband or child without batting an eye if they felt like it, just to provoke them. People walked briskly. St. Bastian's continued to ring out death knells though there were no longer any funeral processions. Families would simply carry off the coffin, dig a grave, and make their way back home under military escort.

Sometimes, Rosa would go downstairs, knock on René's door twice, lightly, and ask him to do something for her husband. Cesare was losing his wits, locked up at home, dying of hunger and fear, burning the last of the firewood. They gave him embroidery samples to keep his hands busy and, after a bit of convincing, he accepted, though he wept giant tears and fidgeted continuously, desperate to go out and bring back some food for Danilo, as a real father would.

The Maremma soldiers were the only ones to come into the workshop but, like the rest of the town, they no longer had the nerve they'd had a few weeks earlier. Recently, René's commissions had been assigned to one young soldier in particular. His name was Simone and he came from the nearby coast. An insipid twenty-two-year-old blond, he had a nervous tic which consisted of blinking all the time. He had been assigned to the villa and was forced to follow Rizziello's orders. Like everyone else, he felt that things were taking a nasty turn. Every three of four days, he would come into the workshop carrying a sack filled with boots, shoes, buckles, belts, holsters, and bags. He would stretch out the errands as an excuse to gain half an hour with the cobbler far away from the dictates and the depressing atmosphere created by the Germans now in charge of the garrison.

René spoke little, measuring every word. There was an ever-present danger that this young soldier has been sent to test him out. He had that impression especially when Simone would take him into his confidence, and come out with things that seemed incredibly reckless. Things like this, for example, "Before I was called up, I thought about cutting two fingers off so I wouldn't make the grade." Given the current climate, an off-the-cuff comment like that was equivalent to high treason. Simone batted his eyelids like a butterfly and dropped bombs such as, "If it were up to me, I would give myself up to the

Allies with open arms," or, "I'd like to be one of those who take back Rome."

René never said anything. He focused on hammering in boot nails and peeling off heels that had soaked so long that they had boiled the soldiers' feet. In between rants, Simone also talked about the war. He sensed the front was moving north and it was like a fever for him. "How are we supposed to shoot against the side we'd like to be fighting for?" he would say. He may have been soft in the head. Saying something like that was grounds for immediate arrest.

The fact of the matter was that the reason Le Case was being so tightly controlled, like everywhere else perhaps, was that the Allies were on their way to rout the Nazis. News came in of landings and carpet bombings. According to Simone, the good news was that the partisans were re-organizing into bigger, more powerful units so that they could contribute to flushing out the enemy. Targets like the villa had taken second place: too great a risk for too little. It was better to play at the grown-up table so that even the small fry would have a role in the victory. Simone was waiting for the wave to move up from the South, even though it would be the end of him. The way things were looking, he didn't have the option to desert: he would be captured and shot on the spot. There were lots of soldiers like him, impaled on the horns of the same dilemma. He would leave the workshop paler than when he came in, begging René to get everything done by the next day.

The names of the soldiers who had sent them in to be mended had been freshly penned on the boot tongues: Donnoli, Carretta, Zucchelli, Passini. All kids. All in the Maresciallo's court. What did they think of the news coming in from Radio Roma? After this earth-shattering reversal, anyone who had made light of the prison camp was in trouble. Even the boys for whom René was hammering nails into boot soles.

He chose rusty nails, some so brittle that they crumbled at the first blow. He hammered them in a little crooked, curved inwards as if he were aiming for the heel. He would use all his skill to drive the nails in as far as the sole so that they would only start to trouble their owner after ten days or more. At which point, they would provoke a calvary of painful barbs.

He pictured the nails, whose tips he was now sharpening with a file, as they started to emerge during a march or while on guard duty; a soldier's step suddenly slowed down by a prick: "Ouch!" And that would be just the beginning; more time would go by before he would be obliged to pay more attention. In the meantime, the hole in the sole would get wider, like a small surface wound. The nails were so rotten that the boot might fall apart at any moment and turn into something resembling a slipper. If the soldier didn't get tetanus, there was still the little matter of a useless pair of clogs. The holes would be manageable for a bit, but if he needed to move on in a hurry, they would be an impediment. He might even trip and fall over. René had used the same technique with nuns' shoes.

The partisans were fighting up in the thick of the woods; he was fighting in his workshop. Had the scared young soldier taken a shine to him? He seemed to be delivering commissions from the villa and from the garrison one at a time. He had even started bringing in gifts. It felt like a genuine act of friendship, but René couldn't get it out of his head that the lad was trying to buy his trust with pieces of cheese and tinned food.

Sometimes he would take the food to the Calò family, making Danilo insanely happy. He didn't tell them about Simone, and only stayed a few minutes. Things being as they were, it would be tempting to spend time together and encourage one another. Rosa once said, "I'll go and get Anna. How can she spend all that time alone in silence?" René explained once again that she wanted it that way; Edoardo's death was still an open wound and commanded all of her time. Germans or no Germans, the only thing she wanted was to wallow in her memories. At the end of the day, it was nothing but the truth.

2

I t was important for Simone to talk. He talked constantly as a way to defend himself from the thoughts that assailed him. René gleaned as much information as he could about the villa.

For example, it appeared that a certain Laura was five months pregnant. And that the prisoners were bored, more than anything else. The men spent their afternoons playing cards or chess. Lunch and dinner were served in the common room. By seven, the lights were out, and at five in the morning they were up doing the cleaning.

Before the Germans took over the military command, the guards under Rizziello had sat at the same recreation tables, leaning their rifles against the wall. Simone had made a name as a top-ranking chess player. Needless to say, friendships had been forged, and there had even been some romantic involvement between a soldier from Scansano and a prisoner from Sovana.

That was all over now. The boys in uniform who had whiled away their time with the inmates until a few weeks before were required to display the same temperament as soldiers from the Wehrmacht. "It's like they're sleepwalking into it," Simone said, squeezing his brain in vain for words to describe the detached manner of the Nazi guards. Unable to find an explanation, he had resorted to magic. "Maybe they're all under a spell," he muttered to himself. "They treat stones better than the prisoners."

René was one of the lucky ones—he didn't have to stay home all day. Because the townsfolk ran the risk of being beaten no matter what they did in Le Case, they had been reduced to two significant actions per day: opening their eyes in the morning and closing them at night. In between these two moments, they had to make an inordinate effort not to go crazy with hunger and worry. There was no way even to know whether other people in their neighborhood were dead or alive. Their view of the world was through a window and they had to make do with the little they could see: the street, the shutters on the building opposite. It wasn't surprising that Cesare Calò was losing his mind sitting at the kitchen window doing nothing except watching the days come and go.

The town had been transformed into a place where people started talking to themselves out loud. If he hadn't had his notebook, René might have caught the bug, too.

Once he had filled both sides, he would tear the page out of the notebook and throw it into the fire. It was painful and pleasurable at the same time. He would watch the paper with fresh ink on it burn and he would be either gripped by a sensation that all was lost, or be filled with courage, as if to say, "Here I am, in the throes of this adventure and I'm staying the course." He liked the idea of sending Anna letters from the fireplace, of words flying out of the chimney and somehow landing in the woods. He pictured a speck of soot landing on Anna's nose, so close it would make her sneeze. That speck would be him.

While poor old Cesare Calò embroidered doilies to keep himself sane, René had invented his secret diary to keep himself going. There were times when he invoked Anna's presence so vividly that he was choked by fear. He couldn't remember her voice. The more he tried to recall it, the more it escaped him, which made him feel like the floor was opening up and swallowing him whole. At other times, he would be busy and suddenly a flash of her doing something perfectly ordinary would come to him, a flash that René treasured and only discovered in that moment of revelation: say, Anna turning suddenly from the stove and serving him some tea, the late evening sun illuminating her forehead. Maybe their friendship had simply been a series of episodes he had stored away that he was now torturing himself with. He could see them, perennially suspended between one conversation and another, pinned down by each other's gazes, as if they were on the verge of unveiling something that would throw them into uncertainty.

In the early days, he had been obsessed with the idea of giving her a kiss. Edoardo had already turned ten. The idea that they might be a couple one day wasn't as shameful as it had been before, especially in the eyes of the town. He had seen women after the first world war who had gone back to popping out kids with new husbands, paying no heed to the scandal. But Edoardo turned twelve, and then fourteen, and nothing changed. The René who rang on the door after work behaved more like an uncle.

There was embarrassment when at the end of the evening he would say, "Right, time's up." Maybe they had talked and drunk a little more than usual. René would wait for a signal, feigning comic maneuvers as he got up from the table and desperately hoping to hear her say, "Stay." But she never did. He contented himself with her slightly pained expression that might have been interpreted as an entreaty.

Anna had waited for him for years and then she had grown tired of it. As time went by, he, too, had fallen into the habit of almost taking her for granted. She hadn't been looking for anyone else, after all. In fact, she had rejected the few men who had fallen for her and had been willing to take on a stepson (like that great worker Gioacchino Rustici, for example, bless his soul). Anna would usher René into her home, dying to pass on the gossip. "Guess who asked me to go to mass with him on Sunday?" She would eliminate every candidate, one after the other, without a yes or no, since after a week it was automatically a no. As if it were a pact. She was holding on to an agreement she had never signed and, in the meantime, continued to reject suitors who could have taken her away from that building and given her a new life close to Le Case, such as up in the Meleta hills. In short, she stayed. She used to joke with him about those upstarts with clods of earth in their teeth, even though she enjoyed being courted. René would go home worse for the drink and look into the mirror he had looked at himself in since he was a boy, his heart thudding. "It must be you she wants," he would say to his reflection. Then he would shake his head. Letting thoughts like that sink into his skull was worse than allowing weeds to fester.

Edoardo turned twenty and René's fingers had still not grown back. He had continued to ask himself the same question until he was worn down by it. If he'd had a normal right hand, a whole strong hand to pick things up with and hold on to them, would it have made a difference? Would he be dragging around the permanent aura of a cripple? Sometimes he would conduct an experiment with Anna: suddenly pulling out his gun, say, and laying it on the table, right there in the open. She would go on bustling about the house as if there was nothing significant in the gesture, which made him burn alive. And René would think, "So, she does see me as being complete!" And then, "If this isn't love, what is?" And yet, he had carried on sitting on the fence. Declaring his love might have created havoc, with Edoardo being forced to move him to a different position on the chess board, among other things. Then one fine day, after so many tragedies and so much emptiness, Anna had flown the coop.

3

S imone was in mid-flow, ranting for the umpteenth time that he had only just understood what was at stake in the war and what side he wanted to be on. News of the Allied landing in Anzio and their thrashing of the Germans was spreading fast. The young soldier was itching for action. The words tumbled out of René's mouth almost without his realizing it. "Give it a rest. Go and join them in the woods."

He knew he had crossed a line and was about to back-tread, but a game was being played: Simone had been weighing up René, but at the same time, René was weighing up Simone. If Rizziello were interrogating him, René would know how to argue his case: the young lad was fragile, clueless, and harbored subversive ideas. He boasted about going to the other side all the time, but was still following orders. René was just provoking him, but there was no way he would he have pushed him into the partisans' arms. How far was the lad willing to go? René was debating all this inside his head when Simone said simply, "How?"

He decided to push him a little further. "Leave at night. The villa is right there by the woods."

Simone thought about it. The possibility lit him up for a moment, giving him a flush of color. Then he was suddenly drained. "At muster, they follow us, and I would be an easy target for the reds in the woods." Then he chuckled. "For God's sake, René, if someone's going to riddle me with bullets, I'd rather it was them."

If he was acting, he was good. For one thing, he had never said anything to suggest he suspected that prisoners from the villa were communicating with moles in the stores and therefore with the partisans. Or had he been waiting for an opening to bring up that very subject? He talked about friends he was no longer allowed to smile at, people he was required to escort to the bathroom, monitoring how long they stayed there. It was during these breaks, Simone had told him, that the prisoners begged him to help them escape, making promises, undertaking to hand over their property in return for a favor, even though their houses had already been requisitioned by government decree. Their property may well have been what Ercolani was counting on to pay the bishop his rent for the villa, after all.

Another of Simone's grievances was the new strategy being rolled out in town. He described how the Germans were suddenly acting like friends. After beating up Farfallina, they were offering bars of chocolate to little girls and old ladies sitting on their stoops getting some air. "They never approach the men, except the priest." The Nazis were using hunger to tame Le Case and the women had fallen hook, line, and sinker into the trap. Not one of them refused the gifts. Maybe out of fear. Or, rather, cunning: they accepted the chocolate and sent it where it was needed, without debating the issue. This didn't mean that in their hearts they didn't wish the garrison would be blown to smithereens one day soon. Nobody should condemn those families who let soldiers into their girls' bedrooms either: was it better to die of hunger or tolerate a daughter taking off her panties out of necessity?

René didn't know why Simone had chosen to share his confidences with him, of all people. Whenever he tried to shake off the idea that they had given the young soldier the task of unmasking him, he always came up with the same answer: he trusted the lad because he felt sorry for him. He was deficient in some way, though he was old enough to wear his father's clothes. What kind of trouble could someone like him cook up?

Simone often talked about two young men: a certain Alberto, and a Renato, which incidentally was René's real name. If they hadn't been locked up in the villa and there hadn't been a war on, Simone said, he would have chosen them as friends to go to town fairs with, looking for girls or a bit of rough and tumble. Until not very long ago, they had been fooling around together, and now he had to follow their every step with a rifle in his hands. They begged and implored him, repeating endlessly that if their roles had been reversed, they would already have found a way to get him out of the camp. They often used the term "friend" and, given the times, the word was as heavy as all the stones in a cathedral. Simone carried the weight around his neck like an accusation, but there was nothing he could do about it. The villa had turned into a place where every gaze was a giveaway, Nazi guards hung out in the common room, and even the light shining in through the big windows seemed to have changed.

Then there was Michele, the other soldier from Saturnia. He was plump and good-natured, with kindness shining in his eyes. René had heard so much about the boy that he felt he almost knew him. He had imagined what he looked like and sometimes he even dreamed about him.

Simone would say, "We've been studying an escape route behind the sentry tower closest to the mountain." There was a spot where the ground had given way and two sections of barbed wire were practically swinging, a legacy of a camp thrown together from one day to the next. But it would be hard to get his two friends that far.

During recreation, Simone and Michele made plans, took note of fault lines, noted guard changes. But there was no follow up. They didn't even tell the two prisoners who had a stake in the matter. They used their strategy meetings to keep their minds busy. Alfredo and Renato were a project that stayed in its rightful place: in their imagination. They did it so that they could go to bed and fall asleep immediately rather than lie there with their eyes wide open, drowning in guilt and fear.

Simone kept beating himself up with questions. "What would happen if one morning word got around that two prisoners had escaped in the night? Who would pay?" Of course, the atmosphere in the camp would turn nasty, both for the Maremma soldiers and for the internees, for whom the consequences would be harsher, of course. Prisoners left behind would pay for the two who had run away, with interrogations, restrictions, and punishments. So, what was the best way to keep the poor prisoners happy and fight for the cause at the same time?

It was after an exchange like this that René put down his ace card, the Settebello that had been his nickname for most of his life. If Simone didn't like it, the cobbler would be dead.

"Boots are my secret weapon in this war," he said.

4.

One evening, Anna had commented, "We don't have an adjective for people from Le Case."
What she meant was that outsiders had no name with which to call them, whereas inhabitants of other towns have an adjective that describes their provenance: Florentine, Pisan, Sienese, you name it. "What are we?" The question drove them both crazy.

Lecasians? Casentines? They tried every combination until they came up with Casinos, though it might have been the drink that had led them to that solution. They burst out laughing, but there was a bittersweet aftertaste that left them feeling unsettled. Having a name was the beginning of everything, and set many other things in motion. And yet, they lived in a place where nobody even wondered why. The more they thought about it, the more invisible they felt, first and foremost to themselves. Not having a precise connotation to be ashamed of is a curse.

René had been thinking back to that conversation when Simone came bursting in, out of breath. He closed the door behind him and said, "We've done it!"

He was like a ball bouncing erratically off the workshop walls. Clapping his hands, he said, "If they catch me, I'll die happy." A second later, he sank into a state of abject terror, then swung back into euphoria.

The news was highly confidential and would never make it past the barbed wire surrounding the camp: Alfredo and Renato had vanished. Michele's head had been down the toilet, puking his guts out since before muster, and he was still there. They blamed the supplies, as there had been some cases of food poisoning. A few weeks before, a stock of canned food had brought the camp to its knees. If the partisans had decided to turn up right then, they would have found the place with no defenses.

"Oh my God!" Simone shrieked, banging his fist on his palm. René warned him to calm down. The boy froze, as if a platoon of Nazis had just walked in. He slumped onto the workbench but he was wound up so tight he was giving out sparks. Just sitting there with his hands in his lap, he was sending out little electric shocks.

They had become partners in crime: days had gone by and René had not been executed yet. Simone knew about the boot tampering, and maybe that was what had made him dare put the plan he and Michele had chewed over for so long into action. Something along the lines of, "If a mutilated cobbler can play a role in the uprising, why can't we young men with rifles?" Now the soldier was dealing with a situation that was making him quiver, curse, and dream. Helping his two friends escape had made him feel like he had achieved something, but he was still on edge because the stakes were high and the jackpot pure gold.

It was the first escape since Ercolani, under German military command, had decided to set up a prison camp in the bishop's villa. The situation was clear: someone must have helped them. There was no way the runaways could have done it on their own. For the Nazis, this was not only an affront. They felt their authority going to the dogs and the whole thing reeked of partisan involvement.

Simone had put on a magnificent show when they had interrogated him, the questions bouncing off him easily. The interpreter had conveyed the meaning of the Germans' snarls and he hadn't missed a beat. The young soldier had stuck to his version: not a leaf had stirred the night he had been on patrol duty. Duty officers from the other three sentry towers had confirmed.

The first sweep produced no results. There had been no trace of Alfredo and Renato outside the villa, not even a broken twig, which told another story: either the prisoners were very skilled, or there had been an accomplice on the other side of the fence. The shadow of the partisans loomed again. In the camp, all eyes were on the woods. A wild boar tripping over a branch was enough to set off an alarm. "I did it all myself," Simone said, as if he couldn't believe his own words. He really hadn't expected such a palaver, with Rizziello out of control after receiving a dressing-down, and the Nazis all of a sudden less cocksure than usual. They had even taken to leaving five of their own guards in the camp overnight.

"Tread carefully," René said. This was the time to keep their antennas up. When things are in disarray, a weak spot can often become as conspicuous as raw skin, which is where you need to sink your teeth in when the right time comes.

"How do you know all this?" Simone asked, growing suspicious, maybe for the first time. He was shocked that a maimed cobbler like him would know about these things.

"That's how it has always been in Le Case," he answered. "A world war is not that different."

5

Although sabotaging boots didn't give immediate results on the war front, it did mean that Simone came back regularly. On one of the tongues, René found the name Carretta. "He's a snake," he heard Simone mutter. He knew the fellow soldier well. "He'd give his mother away to get his finger on a trigger."

Simone was spouting venom, but Carretta had nothing to do with it. René repeated what he had already told him, "It's not your fault." Simone hung his head, ashamed to be seen in the state he was in. He swiped at his tears with his jacket sleeve.

There was something else that would never reach Le Case. Private Michele Tortora had shot himself in the head two days before, after Alfredo, one of the runaways from the seminary, had been found hiding in an old farmhouse near Niccioleta.

"It took two pairs of arms to get him off the truck," Simone said, a wild look in his eye. "I was far away, but even if I'd been right there, I wouldn't have recognized him: cropped hair, different clothes, his face transformed by beatings. I went straight away to look for Michele, but he was nowhere to be seen."

The shot had made the whole villa contingent leap to attention and grab their rifles. The soldiers had spread out, taking up their positions. The gunfire appeared to have come from inside the building, but there was no way anyone could have breached the place. Simone was one of the last to run to the bathroom. He caught a glimpse of Michele's body on its side, a German soldier spitting on it.

Blinking madly, Simone said, "He knew he wouldn't be able to resist the torture if Alfredo revealed anything. Being as good as dead at that point, he decided to shoot himself." He looked at René, a hint of a smile on his face and added, "This may be the last time I can come here."

René knew what he meant, and yet Simone was right there in his workshop, which meant that Alfredo had a thick skin, nerves of steel, and was not talking. Maybe he would keep going until . . . The young soldier shook his head. They were wearing the prisoner down. The Germans couldn't let an opportunity like that escape them. Which soldier had opened the camp gates? Who had helped him in the woods? How did he end up in that farmhouse? Who were the farm workers in contact with? Where were they hiding? What were their plans?

Simone felt like a dead man walking. He leaped out of his skin at every creak, and at night his bed was surrounded by a ring of shadows. "If it goes on much longer, I'll be joining Michele in no time at all." His only defense was to feign normality. A desperate attempt to slip away in the night was not an option. After the escape, they had doubled the guards, and he wouldn't have gotten as far as the entrance hall. Exploiting the prisoners' outings would also have been a novice's mistake: vanishing all day and then failing to show up with your mess tin in the evening would have set the Nazi search parties off with a terribly small handicap. He may as well dig his own grave. Not to mention that venturing into the woods dressed as a soldier was not the brightest move.

The Germans had given orders to dump Michele's body on the lawn as a warning. It was so cold that his flesh didn't rot, but seeing his friend lying there blue in the face was not easy. Simone was not the only one to turn pale. When the crows landed, many of the soldiers felt their own flesh being torn at. They started throwing stones, before expressing their amazement at the turn of events. None of them would ever have thought Michele would be capable of bringing off a plan to help two prisoners escape. As soon as he'd seen one of them being brought back, he had given up the fight without even being charged. "He shouldered all the blame," Simone muttered. "Taking the heat off. For now, at least."

Making his way to the door, he looked as hang-dog as the prisoners. Maybe he was waiting for René to say something to encourage him, but nothing came to René's mind. He thought it a terrible shame that a nice young man like him should have to bear a burden like that. He had actually been on the verge of saying, "Listen, lad. I have a house I've been pretending is inhabited for weeks, but there's nobody there. I can hide you. The Germans may as well go and search for you on the moon." But Simone broke in first, "The other prisoners fared worse than Alfredo, though."

"Which others?"

"The three partisans they caught in the farmhouse. They've locked them up in another wing of the seminary. The one where the bishop sleeps and teaches those two little priests."

"Did you see them?"

"The priests?"

"No, the partisans."

Simone said, "The soldiers had to beat them to get them off the truck. Can you imagine, one of them was a woman."

6

Even so much as an apple would make him puke. All he did was stare at the workshop door, which sat there being a door, although nobody was using it to come in or out. His stomach roiled if he drank a glass of water, but wine went down fine, straight past the brick in his belly. He had to keep an eye on the drinking, as he never seemed to get enough. When he went home, he wouldn't go upstairs. He would stand on the landing expecting to see Anna's band of brothers with handkerchiefs around their necks and a plan for her escape. He dreamed that Mosca would say to him, "We need someone to make a sacrifice," and René would be ready, the pin of a hand grenade in his mouth, ready to blast the villa's gates. But nobody ever came.

It was the worst winter on record. Don Lauro walked through the town in his black tunic looking like the protagonist of a nightmare. That much ice was too much, even for him, as if heaven itself were conspiring to keep everything screwed down tight, what with the war, the rationing, and now the camp. The snow felt like it was upping the ante, deliberately laying on further punishment. The priest went on home visits but felt cheated. All he could do was ring a death knell as a reminder that yet another townsperson had met their end from fever or starvation.

Cesare Calò fainted in the middle of the street as he was looking for Dr. Salghini to come to the house for little Danilo, whose cough was worsening. Nobody went to help him. He lay there with his face in the ice for a good while, with the result that he got a temperature, too. Children and old people risked the most from a bout of bronchitis when they were malnourished. There was no one left in Le Case with enough strength, say, to throw a nice big stone through the windscreen of a military van. People collapsed on the stairs just carrying home a bundle of firewood for the stove.

René discovered that Anna had become his secret weapon. After being inconsolable, something had shifted inside him. The torture of knowing she had been taken prisoner had turned into deep anger. It was what kept his hunger at bay and what staved off the cold. Anger gave him a measure of everything he was doing; it guided both his thoughts and his good hand as he wrote pages and pages that went up the chimney. Maybe he'd gone mad. If he had, it was a gleaming sort of madness that made him feel as sharp as a knife blade. Imagining Anna being manhandled was so offensive that it made him feel prepared for any ordeal. Not like a hothead who jumps blindly into the fray. No, his breathing was steady and his heart was still. It might have been how Anna felt after Edoardo's execution. She had thrown herself into the breach to save herself from heartbreak. Now it was his turn.

7

Maresciallo Rizziello went straight to the point. "René, I've heard you've been buying more than your share of pencils and notebooks lately. It makes me wonder, when there are folks who struggle to put one meal a day on the table."

One of the three soldiers he had brought with him was standing at the workshop door. The other two flanked their ranking officer like guardian angels.

René attempted a smile. "Is it a crime?" He had aimed to make it sound like a sincere question, but it came out wrong, with an insolent ring to it.

Rizziello studied the cobbler for a moment then nodded at the young lad on his right, the red-head, who clicked his heels and took something out of his jacket pocket. He handed it over to his superior. It was his notebook.

"Excuse me, where did you get that from?" René asked, knowing full well there was no point. They had clearly been in his apartment.

Rizziello opened the cover. There were only a few pages left inside; no more than ten. Flipping through the blank pages with his thumb, he said, "So, what's this then?"

René was quick to defend himself. "Sir, it's just that . . . Well, basically, I quite like writing and . . . "

"Are you thinking of writing a novel, René? What's it about?"

The street suddenly went dark as a truck pulled up outside the workshop.

"No, of course not. In the evening, I sit by the fire and write down my thoughts. It's something I've taken up recently to keep me company. Random stuff. It helps me pass the time."

Rizziello stared back at him. "We've looked everywhere. There's no trace of these notes anywhere in your apartment. Do you know what that made me think?"

René shook his head.

"It made me think that these blank sheets here are what remain of the many messages you've been sending who knows where."

"Messages? Who would I send messages to?"

"You tell me."

René opened his eyes wide in dismay. "Sir, you don't actually think that I—"

"So, where are the pages you have written?"

"In the fireplace!"

"In the fireplace?"

"I write about the past, keeping myself going with a bit of wine, so that I can get to sleep more easily. Writing down my memories makes me feel better. The problem is that when I wake up the next day, I'm ashamed. The drivel that ends up on paper when I'm a little tipsy is beyond belief. Romantic escapades and stuff like that from a lifetime ago that I hardly remember the next day. If any of it were to end up in the wrong hands . . . No, it doesn't bear thinking about."

"So, you're writing love letters?"

"Well, I wouldn't call them that exactly."

"Declarations of love, then? You know the kind? The kind of words for a woman we've loved in secret but have never had the courage to express because we've always been too cowardly."

"Whatever, it all ends up in the fire."

"Because it takes courage to love. Isn't that true for everyone, René?"

"Maybe, but I've never . . . "

"Take Anna, for example. The town folk say you're very fond of one another. The Calò family upstairs have confirmed this."

"We've always been good friends."

"When was the last time you saw her?"

"Anna? I don't know. Maybe four or, at the most, five days ago. Once a week I do a spot of shopping for the both of us, if there's anything to buy, of course. I have her permission to pick up her rations. Anna doesn't like going out much. Why are you asking?"

"Her apartment was spic and span."

"What do you mean?"

"There wasn't a thing out of place. The floors are as shiny as mirrors."

"Did you pay her a visit?"

"It was like going into a house that had not been lived in. Not a speck of dust anywhere."

"Well, that's how my friend passes her time, with a duster at the ready at all times."

"The fire was out. How do you explain that, René?"

"Maybe she's saving wood? With a winter like this . . . "

"It's been out for days. That was immediately clear."

"No, that's not possible. She's not completely off her head."

"There wasn't so much as a lump of old cheese in the larder."

"Sir, our rations are hardly enough for one person to live on; we don't have any leftovers these days."

Rizziello suddenly looked tired, as if he had lost steam. He gestured to the soldiers. "Go on, arrest him." He said it as if he had been devoured by boredom.

René's world collapsed. "What?"

Rizziello raised his hand to stop the redhead from grabbing the cobbler. "Listen, let's be clear here."

"Sir, honestly, I . . . "

"Who do you see in front of you?"

"Sir, I see you. Sir!"

"And who am I?"

"You are Maresciallo Gaetano Rizziello, sir. Everyone knows that. Why were you saying. . . ?"

"A high-ranking officer from the town garrison takes the bother to step into a hole like this. What does that make you think?"

" . . . "

"There you are. Silence is the best answer. Let's stop the nonsense now."

"Sir, not for one second have I ever . . . "

"She has talked."

"What?"

"Your great friend, hiding out with the communists, captured last Friday with a few other partisans and a runaway from the camp. She has talked."

"I'm sorry, but I don't understand what you're . . . "

For a moment, Rizziello looked as though he had fallen for René's incredulity. He glanced down at the cobbler's mangled hand: anyone could see that someone like him would never have been able to take the initiative. It was as absurd as if it suddenly rained upwards.

He leaned forward and gave him a pat on the back. "Don't worry, René," he said. "Someone will make you talk." Then, turning back to the soldiers, he told them to take him away.

THE BISHOP'S VILLA

1

If Anna really had talked, they would have eaten him alive right away, but all they had done was lock him up. His German guard was skinny and bald, with engorged veins at his temples: he would come in, pick up his bowl, and leave.

René had been a guest at the villa for three days and nobody had asked him a single question. They had simply left him in that room in his underpants and vest. To humiliate him, but also so that he would feel the cold nipping at him. At one point, he had said to the scrawny guard, "If I catch my death, I'll be no use to you." The German closed the door gently, almost without a sound.

His toilet bucket was picked up by a soldier from Maremma who had been assigned to that wing of the villa. He came in twice a day: once in the morning and once in the evening. The lad was well trained, and never responded, even to a "good day." René would stare at him and, after a while, the soldier would feel the prisoner's eyes on him and shoot a glance back, only to look straight down again. It was a strange connection, as if for a moment it had become apparent to them that they were both prisoners. Both felt a vice at their throat under the icy gaze of their superior in polished boots at the door.

They were on the first floor of the residence. The room was spacious, nothing like a cell, except for the bars that had been added to the windows. It may have been a guest room or the servants' quarters in the old days. A chair and a bucket, no bed. The door was a normal wooden door, floor tiles made of marble chips. The only embellishment was a bare crucifix with a dried olive branch attached to it.

At times, it felt as if he'd been dropped there in a dream. He would rub his eyes and ask himself, "Is this really happening?" Searching for a sign that it was true, he would look down at the pistol shape of his maimed hand. If this had been a dream, it would have been the first thing he would have changed. Instead, there it was in his lap.

Then there were waves of dread that were so overpowering he would start snorting like a bull. At times, it was hard to control himself. He wanted to kick and scream. Luckily for him, a flame burned inside him, reminding him to stay the course, exactly where he was: on a chair in a room of the seminary, fighting the battle he had been sucked into.

He had never stopped writing, only now he did it in his head. The aim was no different: to speak to his friend, Anna. He worked so hard at it that he built a bridge. Or rather, a thread. He imagined it so clearly that he could almost see it. A thread that, first from his notebook, and then from his thoughts, would become more tangible, reducing the distance between them day by day until they would finally meet again face to face.

2.

Assigned to Rizziello was a certain bootlicker named Ciavatti, whose blond hair and bland features would have been the envy of a Nazi. In fact, he did everything to imitate their manner, adopting a stern expression and a permanent snicker, somewhere between revulsion and scorn. He lit a cigarette, then sat there for a while, leaning back in the chair behind the metal desk, contemplating the bright light pouring in through the big windows. For a moment, René couldn't see him for the thick, white smoke. Without looking at him, the officer said, "Did you sleep well?"

René had been pulled out without warning. Walking down the corridors, he caught sight of himself in a mirror. His nose was out of place and his face, in general, did not look like his own. Whenever he shifted his gaze, the information came in with a fraction of a delay. Moving his mouth, he was unsure whether his jaw would follow his commands. All he felt was a dull, pulsating ache from his forehead down to his chin.

"No," he said.

Ciavatti shifted in his seat and it creaked. He rested his cigarette on the ashtray, which made a little rainbow refraction. Finally, he looked at the prisoner. He didn't look remotely shocked to see him in that condition. "Any thoughts?"

René didn't know whether it was possible to faint in your sleep, but somehow he had ended up covered in blood. He smelled it, felt its stickiness and the pain. He had lain on the floor crying, calling out for help, maybe fainting again, until first light. All of a sudden, a pail of cold water had been poured over him. Then two men had pulled him to his feet.

Although it was hard to speak, he'd said, "You should be ashamed of yourselves."

The officer picked up his cigarette again and took a drag. Then he nodded at the German standing at the door, who turned on his heels and left the room. Another guard stood behind René.

"Nobody is enjoying themselves here. At the end of the day, it's you who—"

The prisoner was racked by coughs and dark splotches of spit flew onto some papers on the desk. "Jesus," Ciavatti exclaimed, but René couldn't stop. Dense globs of blood and snot kept on coming. The chair swung back and was dragged to a safe distance. Rizziello's little helper stared at the prisoner with repugnance, waiting for the coughing fit to abate.

When it finally did, René was panting and felt a whistling in his ear. The officer threw a rag of some kind into his lap. René took it and wiped his mouth, staining the cloth red.

"Let's go back to the beginning," Ciavatti said. "How did you send messages?"

Rene's shortness of breath and heart palpitations had not passed. Neither had his nausea. "I never wrote any messages. They were just memories."

The officer was annoyed. "René, do you really expect me to believe you sent love letters up the chimney?"

"That's exactly what I did."

Ciavatti smiled. He looked like the devil. "You're not getting the point. If you collaborate now, we'll forget everything. We know perfectly well that a cobbler is not going to be a kingmaker for the Resistance. You've just been taken in by those doe eyes. Let's have a nice chat now, shall we? Then I'll tell them to take you home. Look at you. You need some rest."

René realized that tears were rolling down his face, mixed

in with the snot. He didn't want to cry, but he couldn't help it. "I've done nothing wrong."

Ciavatti sighed. "What can you tell me about Anna?"

"You murdered her son."

"That boy signed his own death sentence when he deserted. And his mother stayed in contact with the partisans, right? Give me some names and I swear that by midday today, you'll be having lunch by your damned fireside. You have my word."

"I don't know what you're talking about."

Ciavatti leaned back in his chair. He looked up. There was a commotion behind the prisoner. Steps. Then a second chair. A body was dumped into it. The first thing René noticed were the man's filthy, bare feet. Trying to move his neck to look up, pain coursed through his body, but he finally managed to see the man's face.

Under the layer of beatings, he recognized Mosca. With no glasses and thin as a rake. Emaciated lips. René smothered his face in the rag.

"René, who is this man?"

"I don't know."

"Are you sure? Look properly."

René didn't say anything.

The same question was asked of the young partisan. "Do you know who this man is?"

Mosca cleared his throat. "His name is René. You just said it yourself, you Fascist pig."

Ciavatti gave a signal to one of the German soldiers standing behind them. A fist came down on Mosca, just above his ear. Caught by surprise, he fell off the chair and the room echoed with the crack of his head hitting the floor. The guards threw themselves onto him right away and propped him back up in the chair.

The officer tried again. "Who is this man?"

Mosca smiled, but it was clearly forced. He, too, had been betrayed by an uncontrolled tear drop. The partisan was about to say something else, for which he would certainly be punched again; it was a sight that René did not want to witness. "Sir," he volunteered. "It's the first time I—"

A white flash and the room disappeared. For a few seconds, he didn't even know whether he had a body or which way was up. He was shaken. He could only see the officer in flashes. His head was on fire. Dark, almost black, drops fell onto the back of his hand. "Help," he heard himself gasp. He tried to move and everything wavered. A tight grip was holding him down.

Mosca was saying things but the words tripped over one another, as if there had been ten of him repeating the same phrase at different times. Meanwhile, the mist was lifting, sucked up by the light coming from the window. Blinking, he managed to regain his focus on the room and the sounds around him. "You can't treat me like this," he whined, sounding like somebody else.

Ciavatti shrugged, "We can do what we like."

"In a month's time, I'll be pissing on your grave," Mosca said. "They're on their way."

It wasn't clear whether he was referring to the Allies or Boscaglia's band of partisans. In any case, the Fascist soldier resumed his habitual sneer. He looked up and nodded at one of the guards. One second later, Mosca had a bag over his head. A plump German came at him from behind and grabbed the prisoner by the wrists as he kicked and screamed.

René was still a little lightheaded, but he instinctively struggled to get onto his feet. Strong hands shoved him back down onto the chair. "What are you doing? Have you gone mad?"

Ciavatti bided his time. He took another deep drag and let out yet another cloud of white smoke. "What can you tell me about this lad?"

Mosca was still struggling, but he was growing weaker and probably wouldn't have been able to stand on his own.

The bag over his head was being sucked in.

"Sir, for the love of God."

"René, it's up to you."

"You'll kill him if you go on."

"Tell me something I don't know."

All of a sudden, Mosca's legs went out from under him, but his upper body was still struggling. Maybe he had momentarily lost consciousness. René yelled with all his strength. "Bastards! Let him go!"

Ciavatti acted as though he were smoking a cigarette between courses in a restaurant. "This is how we deal with prisoners who won't give us any information."

"For heaven's sake, I'm begging you . . . "

"Who is this lad, René? Where is his gang of thugs hiding?"

Mosca's body jerked, turned stiff as a board, and then sagged. The big soldier dropped him, as if the prisoner's wrists were on fire, so that the partisan's arms were hanging limply by his side.

The silence that ensued was like the end of the world. Even the soldiers didn't seem to expect it, including the one pinning down the cobbler who had loosened his hold. René said, "What have you done?"

Ciavatti didn't take his eyes off him. "It's your fault."

The sack was pulled off Mosca's head. On the dead man's face was an expression of bewilderment that was almost beautiful, like the astonished face of a child at the circus. "What have you done?" René repeated, tears and snot running down his face.

Ciavatti glanced at his watch. "What if your lady friend had been in this young man's place?" he said, stubbing out his cigarette. He stood up. "Think about it." He looked towards the door. "Take him away."

More soldiers came in. From the corner of his eye, René saw the ones in Nazi uniform march out before feeling a different pair of hands on his shoulders. "Come on, move," he heard the guard say. Somehow they pulled him to his feet. As he turned around, he saw which soldier it was that had come to fetch him: Simone. Propping him up, he squeezed René's elbow.

Every time he heard the door open it was almost a deliverance after spending every minute of every day waiting for a key to rattle in the lock. They left him in that condition because they knew he would soon be begging them to take him to the chopping block to put an end to the whole thing once and for all.

The blows hurt more than before. His face was a mask of bruises and bumps and a fit of coughing was enough to make him faint. At least they had given him a pair of pants, a rough cotton shirt, and a pair of shoes with no laces that were too big for him. In the morning, they would bring him an old sponge and a bowl of cold water with hairs and other debris floating in it, and the German guard would often spit in it for good measure before leaving it with him. He seemed to take pleasure in the action.

René could see the woods from his window. If there was one good thing, it was that the ice was beginning to loosen its grip. A few days of sunshine had melted the piles of snow and, here and there, green buds had started to appear at the tips of the trees. Le Case had had it bad that year, and it wasn't over yet, for sure. It must have been a relief for the band of partisans, though. Or was the mud slowing them down, maybe? He pictured them in the thick of the woods, carrying out their mission, communicating with mirrors from one peak to another.

Never in his life had he looked out at the peak with as much love, as if it were his own child. The feeling took his breath away. His face was wrecked and he was locked up in the bishop's villa, yet he had been reborn as part of that youthful brigade, prepared to be killed and to spit in the Fascist monster's face. Like Edoardo, the boy he had brought up. Like Mosca. He would rather run to the woods than live in a world with people like Rizziello and Ercolani. He would rather stay in that room, where he washed his face with the spit of Nazi thugs. They were so stupid: the more they tried to scare him, the braver he became. What can you do to a man who looks at you calmly when you threaten him with death? You can chew his bones clean, but you can't touch his soul, which means you will never win.

He no longer had those evenings at the kitchen table with a flask of wine, but talking to Anna in this way was even better. He communicated using silence, anticipation, and interminable nights. His anger seeped through the walls. He hugged her tight, in an embrace he had never been brave enough to give her. And she hugged him back.

A couple of soldiers came in. He had seen them escorting prisoners into town back then, when everything had started. They were followed by a German guard with a whip, like Leonilde Cacciaferri's. He barked an order, pointing at a corner of the room. René moved there.

As usual, the soldiers in the Maremma contingent were expected to do all the work. First, they moved a table. Then they produced two jute sacks which they opened on the table. René recognized his tools immediately: cutters, knives, plyers, dies, fasts, awls. His nail and glue jars. They laid everything out roughly and the curly-haired soldier said, "Is anything missing?"

René was on cloud nine at seeing his tools again, but for a moment, the idea that Ciavatti was so perverse he might want to torture him with his own work tools flashed through his mind. He answered the soldier with another question. "What do you mean?"

The other soldier, who was nearly bald at twenty and boasted a giant strawberry birthmark on his forehead, said, "Maresciallo Rizziello says to give you what you need to get back to work."

Curly-head insisted, "Do you need anything else?"

René cast a glance at the German standing by the door and ventured a step in the Italian soldier's direction. There was no growl. "I'm supposed to repair shoes, in here?"

They didn't answer; there was enough evidence. Curly-head was growing weary. "So, Granddad?"

He suddenly cottoned on to who he was: the soldier who had been so desperate to find out about the girls in town. The one who had acted as though he was on vacation. It seemed so long ago that, in the meantime, his face had turned into parchment. "It depends on what I need to do," René said. "For example, I don't see my rasps, patterns, or cutters."

"You can tell the person in charge."

The young soldiers turned on their heels and left, but the German stayed where he was. His holster was open and his hand was hovering over it, as if he were begging René to make a dash for him brandishing one of the blades lying there on the table.

The bald soldier came back with a sack that he dumped on the floor. "In the meantime, there's this."

The German guard was losing his temper watching him standing there doing nothing and snarled at him, so René advanced hesitantly, unable to shake off the suspicion that the whole charade was a trap. Inching forward, he finally reached the sack, bent over, and untied the lace. He extracted a pair of boots and put them on the table. There was the name Colella G. penned onto the tongue. He could see right away how the soldier must thump his heels and imagined a leaden-stepped, fat hulk who had put so much weight on the back of the boot that the sole had come unstuck in the middle. There was only one way to see how much damage there was, though: he needed a hammer. He had to bang the boot on its side to see how far the sole had become detached, then stick a pen into the gap to test its resistance.

The German didn't flinch when the cobbler reached with his good hand for the mallet. René felt a shock run down his back as he picked it up. Then he got on with the job. The first thud echoed around the room, vibrating even more loudly in his bones. Then came the second. And the third.

He imagined the hammering as a message for Anna, saying, "I'm here, don't worry about a thing."

The strikes said, "We're in this battle together."

Twenty minutes later, the German guard was already yawning. He stood on the threshold but his attention was drawn to the corridor, where he begged every fellow soldier passing by to have a conversation with him. They were all busy doing something else and marched straight on after exchanging a few pleasantries. In his bid for more attention, he spent longer in the corridor than he should have. As the steps faded into the distance, he would sigh deeply as if to say, "Trust my luck to be dumped with guarding a cobbler." He smoked cigarette after cigarette, which he stubbed out on the floor.

Behind the guard, René could see a door on each side of the corridor. In the distance, there was a corner and a right turn, where a nice big window let in the early afternoon sun. Halfway down the corridor, a low table and two little gilded arm chairs had been placed, a painting hanging above them. The doors were all the same, exactly like the one to his cell, and they were all closed. He pretended he was having a coughing fit, even though the pain was excruciating, as if his face were about to be detached, leaving his skull exposed. He didn't care. He would gladly have sneezed until his head fell off if it meant Anna might hear his voice.

Low clouds had shrouded the mountains in dense fog. This happened often in Le Case, even in the summer. All of a sudden, everything would be erased, as if to remind the townsfolk what they were: that is, nothing. The unexpected greyness changed the light and gave the German guard the sensation that his day had been wasted standing there in a doorway. He was so bored he would gladly have shot himself in the mouth.

Colella, meanwhile, was taking a break under the clamps waiting for the glue to dry. René was now dealing with Losurdo: women's slip-ons that might well have belonged to a nun with an uneven gait, maybe a slight limp. The inner and outer soles were so worn out that he could see the metal reinforcement. If she had been a paying customer, he would have said, "Madam, it's not worth the expense; you'd be better off saving up for a new pair."

The truth was that Rizziello didn't know what to do with him, so he had put him to work. He may have harbored the idea that René would secretly be thankful for some clothes and having his workshop at the prison camp so that he could distract himself rather than brooding minute by minute over what awaited him. The Maresciallo was providing the villa with a service while ensuring the prisoner couldn't send messages, if he really thought that's what René had been doing. This made one thing patently obvious: the cobbler was irreplaceable.

Simone came into his room accompanied by a tall, lanky lad in civies with a big nose, who looked so tired he appeared almost tipsy. Simone turned to the German and said, "I'm here to change guard and to find out whether the prisoner needs anything else to carry on working."

The giraffe standing beside him translated. The German absorbed the message and his face slowly lit up. He couldn't wait to desert his post and nodded frantically, emitting a string of words that sounded like farts. Then he patted Simone on the chest and walked out without giving the prisoner so much as a backward glance.

René looked over at Simone's skinny companion and, all of a

sudden, a miracle of sorts took place: a smile, or something like it, began to unfurl on the boy's face. The cobbler could have burst into tears; he accepted the offering as if it were a crust of bread that would bring him back to life. "That's enough for me," he said to himself. He had reached the point where a man looking at him and half-smiling was enough to heal all the hardship, anxiety, and pounding he had suffered.

"You can stand down now," Simone said to the beanpole.

René was sorry to see him go. He stood there dazed, watching the boy's slow progress down the corridor, his arms hanging by his side. As he was walking away, something else unusual happened: he stopped in front of the side table and reached up to straighten the painting on the wall. René couldn't explain why, but it suddenly felt as though the entire revolution might be encapsulated in that gesture.

"René," he heard, only then snapping out of his reverie. As he studied the thrashing René had received, Simone's face creased into an amused grin, "You're off your head," he said. "Nobody's stopping us now."

4.

I t's about two hundred paces," Simone said. "I've counted them, including the two flights of stairs with ten steps each." His gaze shifted to the ceiling. "They're practically on top of us, or one room off either way."

René looked up. After all this, Anna was living above him, rather than the other way around. He was momentarily overwhelmed by how close she was. Simone was riding the wave. He wanted to make the most of his guard duty to get the ball rolling.

"The mood is pretty dark in the camp. Rizziello has arrested Penna for bringing soldiers news from the front. Who knows where he gets it from? For example, we heard that the Resistance is intensifying in the North and that it will soon be ramping up in central Italy. We may be cut off from the rest of the world up here, but in the vast Apennine forests between the Tyrrhenian and the Adriatic coasts, new brigades are springing to life everywhere."

When he was excited, Simone would sometimes change register and use fancy phrases he must have heard on somebody's lips and stolen, like, "We will flourish again as an independent and combative nation." Then there was the bombing of Cassino and the advancing Allied army through the ruins. These felt like distant events and yet they were almost knocking on their door up there in the villa.

The officers of the Wehrmacht shot looks like missiles and meted out harsh punishments on the slightest pretext. The

Maremma contingent of soldiers was under pressure, on a razor's edge every day. Simone felt it, too. He forced himself to adopt an iron fist with the prisoners and followed orders without batting an eye. The Nazis were hurting on all fronts and anything could tip them over the edge. They saw enemies lying in wait even when they looked in the mirror. "It's a good time to attack," Simone said. He was no longer the only rebel in their ranks: his fellow soldiers didn't talk about it, but their eyes spoke volumes. While a few months before they had experienced the war as a kind of vacation, now they realized on what side of the barricade they had been thrust. All of a sudden, the bishop's villa was populated by young men whose conscience had been redrawn from one day to the next. They were like children lost in the wood and the Germans sensed it.

It was worse for the prisoners, who were the designated victims of the Blackshirts' intolerance. You could hear a pin drop in the canteen and common room. The waiting and the anger had worn everyone down. "The villa is like a giant pot coming to the boil," Simone said. "And the lid is about to blow off." He dreamed of being the one who would finally trigger a revolt, pitting converted soldiers and prisoners alike against the Nazis. "The villa is our Monte Cassino," he murmured, biting the inside of his cheek impatiently.

Simone's vehemence scared René. And, anyway, things were different now. Saving Anna was his top priority, while Simone was still pondering ideals. He couldn't say it, of course. If anything, he had to keep that hothead warm, but not too warm, otherwise the young soldier would get so wound up he might march outside on his own with a loaded gun. Even the idea of martyrdom fired him up and it was then that René understood: Simone had crossed the line. His readiness for anything increasingly seemed like madness. His fascination with danger made him behave like a berserk horse. Getting himself assigned to the cobbler was further proof of his propensity for risk. He had simply asked the German commanding officer. After all, he had been the soldier in charge of delivering the boots. Simone swore he had chosen just the right moment and nobody had given a second thought to his request. He may have been right, but it was just as probable that he was wrong. In any case, he was leaving behind a trail of evidence: what twenty-year-old soldier in his right mind would choose to die of boredom guarding an old man suspected of being in cahoots with Boscaglia's brigade? A Nazi might wonder one day. Flapping his hand in the air, Simone swore he had the situation in hand. The German command had placed their own soldiers in strategic positions and Simone had been watching the guard who had been posted there without much conviction. Listening to him describe his maneuvers, anyone would think Simone deserved a special mention for initiative.

At the end of his shift, Simone ordered the cobbler to put all his tools back into the sack. Nothing was to stay out, not even the glue. Likewise, the repaired boots and the ones waiting to be fixed were to be put away until the following day, when work would resume. Once René said, "Why do you need to guard me? I could easily carry on . . . all I would need is a candle." In short, working on the boots would help him get through the night.

Simone smiled. "The soldiers assigned here have only one task: to make sure the prisoners don't kill themselves. Your table is laden with cutters, files and mallets. None of that funny stuff, d'you hear me?"

René watched him leave with the sack, just as he had walked out of the workshop so many times. Except the young soldier walking away now had nothing in common with the pale, anxious lad seeking comfort only a few weeks before. He had changed skin.

5

The sentry tower searchlight lit up the room at intervals. René hoisted his chair onto the table and stood there for a while, staring at the tower. Then he took his shoes off.

It was not an easy climb. The chair didn't look like a model of stability. And what would people think if they found him on the floor with his head cracked open? There was nothing to hold onto. When the searchlight turned away, he felt completely unprotected; when it shone back, there was no improvement as the shadows playing on the walls made him feel dizzy. In the end, he managed to get both feet onto the seat of the chair, his hands gripping the back. He let go abruptly and stood straight, as if he were following a thread that he had created in his mind. Then he stretched out his good hand. He had to stand on tiptoe to reach the ceiling.

Knock.

The first tap of his knuckles was as feeble as a mouse's sneeze. He tried again.

Knock.

The sound was more substantial this time. If there had been a guard at the door, he would have reached for his keys. René wouldn't have been able to get down and tidy everything up even if he wanted to. But nothing happened.

Attempting to stay upright while measuring his strength, he gave two quick raps.

Knock knock.

He tapped again. Then listened.

The muscles in his arms and legs were beginning to burn.

Once more: *Knock knock.*

The searchlight sent an oblique shaft of light across the room just as he was getting his breath back and resting his arms. It felt as though the shadows were about to tip his chair over and he momentarily lost his balance. He saw himself toppling over, making a hell of a racket, and the Nazis ready to finish him off with their batons.

Knock knock.

It wasn't him tapping.

"Anna," he gasped. He was up like a flash, rapping on the ceiling. *Knock knock.*

She answered right away: *Knock.*

To which, he countered: *Knock knock.*

Knock.

Knock knock.

Knock.

They went on like this, René with two taps and Anna with one. Who knew what they were saying after all this time and the thousand adventures that separated them? And yet there was an unstoppable tide of talk.

Knock knock.

Knock.

He could have gone on forever, because it felt like a never-ending embrace, but he heard an order, or something sounding like one, outside together with a scurrying noise that froze him to the chair. He only realized his heart had been beating as fast as a train once he'd managed to bend down and grip the back of the chair. He placed first one foot, then another, on the table and finally landed on the floor, peering cautiously into the penumbra. He was overcome by a sense of giddiness once he realized both feet were on the ground and had to lean on the table as if he were drunk.

The pleasure of having spoken to her was trilling inside him. He sat in his usual corner hugging his knees and looking up. "You're here," he said. Blood coursed through him; he even felt a fever rising. "I'm here," he added.

Knock. He closed his eyes. As if he hadn't closed them since Anna had left.

The rattling caught him by surprise. Chilled to the bone, at the second turn of the key he was already on his feet. Leaping up so quickly after lying still for hours caused a stab of pain to shoot from his neck down to his heels. The fourth turn was like an execution. He was still a few steps away from the table and the chair still perched there. When the German opened the door, he found René holding onto the chair legs. The guard uttered a string of eructations as he looked around in alarm. The water in the bowl that was propped on his chest was rippling.

Everything looked normal: the room, the bucket. There was nothing else. The only addition had been the table, but the German had grown used to it. Looking like a dozy old wolf, he stared at René, who was busying himself with one of the chair legs, scraping at the tip with his fingernail. Knowing the Nazi wouldn't understand a thing, he muttered, "Maybe I can fix it with a hammer. This chair wobbles."

The guard must have understood something. His riposte was to snort like a pig. René said, "For the love of God, please don't . . . " The guard took a step forward and placed the bowl on the table. After a series of revolting grunts, he managed to bring up a giant glob of mucus that formed a long viscous thread as he spat into the dirty water. Words that sounded like a saw grating against stone were the condiments: the Nazi was clearly inviting him to make his morning ablutions.

René clenched his teeth and angrily thrust his hands into the bowl. He grabbed the bar of soap and started scrubbing, churning the water into a tidal wave. If he could disintegrate the glob of phlegm, at least it wouldn't be visible and he would be able to wash his face without retching. Simone appeared when he was halfway through his routine. He smiled one of his nice smiles and, looking at the Nazi, said, "Good morning, piece of shit."

René almost fell into the bowl, but Simone surprised him: he put on a scowl fit for an evil gangster and started railing against him. "Don't worry. If they don't know the words, you can say what you like."

The tone Simone had adopted satisfied the German, who didn't bat an eye. Soldiers were expected to speak harshly to prisoners. René threw water on his face with his hands: phlegm or no phlegm, a splash of icy water was exactly what he needed. In the meantime, Simone had gone to get the sacks and had brought them inside. Finally, he took out a pack of cigarettes and offered one to the Nazi. "Disgusting snake," he said conspiratorially.

The guard thanked him with a nod. He stuck the cigarette between his teeth without lighting it. Then he turned to the prisoner, took the bowl away from under him, without a care for whether René had finished rinsing himself off. As he left, he gave a half-salute to Simone, who countered with a heart-felt, "Your mom's a whore." He might have gone too far: the insult was not exactly uncommon among soldiers after a drink or two. For a moment, it looked as though the guard was slowing down and about to come to a halt, but he didn't. He carried on, humming to himself. Simone waited until he was sure the Nazi had turned the corner before bursting out excitedly, "Did you see that?"

René didn't like it one bit. War should not be waged as if you were fooling around in a tavern. Being reckless like that was for half-wits: for the sake of a joke, you could end up getting shot. And anyway, where would calling the Nazi a son of a bitch get them? He couldn't tell Simone, but the little show he had put on was further proof that he was throwing all caution to the wind. As René was drying his hands with his shirt cuffs, he heard the young soldier say, "René, you haven't heard the news!"

René laid out his work tools on the table without looking at Simone once. As he did so, he listened to news from the front: it had been an unprecedented rout. The Allies had taken two mountains in the area of Cassino, but that was not all. The Germans were having problems in Anzio, too. "Everyone is talking as if it's a done deal," Simone whispered, under the spell of his own words. René abruptly put an end to his ravings. "I spoke to her."

Unprepared, Simone flinched. "Her who?"

René tossed his eyes at the ceiling. "Anna."

The boy must have thought the cobbler had lost his mind. "Really?" he asked. "What did you talk about?"

"Everything."

6

Every now and again, he would wonder how his disappearance had been interpreted in town. Did they think he had joined the ranks of all those others for whom the bells of St. Bastian's had tolled a grim funeral knell? It was unlikely as, one fine day, the Germans had broken into his workshop and collected all his work tools. The last people to see him had been the Calò family, who had been at their door bringing in their usual supplies and hadn't bothered to ask him a thing. Le Case must be shoeless.

Days at the villa chased each other like lightning bolts, with Simone stuck at the door of René's cell when he would have been much happier taking on the world. News from his unknown sources made him feel he was rotting away in there. "The bulletins only ever mention patrols," he would say. "What are we supposed to do with paltry patrols?" He wanted news of breaches, boots marching over the bodies of Germans as they gained territory on their way north. The deadlock was draining his energy and, if he lost that, fear would creep back in its place. He wasn't equipped to deal with emotions, he needed rage fueled by passion, without which he turned into a wet dishrag with dark thoughts. And the villa would suddenly close in on him again.

The fact that René had been imprisoned there was a blessing for Simone, though he wouldn't acknowledge it. Guarding the cobbler allowed him to ramble on and, every now and again, rekindle the fire inside him that he feared had burnt out. The flame revived especially when he insisted on drawing up plans to defeat the Germans and to send a clear signal to the rest of Italy that Maremma was playing its part in the war effort. He was not a day over twenty but, all of a sudden, his greatest ambition was to have ballads written about him. And yet, he was stuck there. When he could take it no longer, he would slump into the gilt-legged chair that he had moved from the passageway to the door of René's cell and bite his nails.

Rizziello's silence, on the other hand, was eloquent: they had not brought the escaped prisoner, Renato Cappelli, back in to squeeze more information out of René. Holding the cobbler there and making him work for them was enough. They had used Mosca to scare him—the young partisan would have been killed anyway. They were holding him until the right moment in a jail cell that was actually an antechamber, a waiting room.

"Have you thought about it?" René asked Simone out of the blue.

Simone twitched as he came out of a light slumber. It was rare for the cobbler to initiate a conversation. First, he looked around him, then he said, "About what?"

"Imagine the Allies routing the Germans on all fronts."

Simone grew animated instantly. "I think about nothing else."

"They are advancing rapidly northwards. Once they liberate Rome, it will be Civitavecchia, then Tarquinia, up, up along the coast. Then they will get to the gates of Grosseto."

"René, my dick is getting hard thinking about it."

"What'll happen?"

Simone sat there looking dumb, then he suddenly came to life. "I'll tell you what'll happen. We'll pile up all the Germans and light a bonfire under them, and then—"

"You're a soldier in the regular army."

Simone looked offended. "That's why I keep saying we need to get going. I don't want to be caught out in this uniform. At least you're a prisoner. Remember, we're in the same boat here. I'm trapped somewhere I don't want to be just as much as you are."

"The big question is what will Ercolani do if he finds out they are right on top of him?"

Simone chuckled. "I can just see him jumping ship like a rat and scuttling away somewhere. Same for that louse, Rizziello. I want to be there when it happens."

They stood there for a while, each conjuring up their own picture of the situation. Then the young soldier said, "So?"

"All I can say is that, if the Nazis beat a retreat, everyone in the regular army will be left in their underpants. Officers and privates will be rounded up. Or forced to run into the woods, which are pretty crowded these days."

Simone blanched. "I won't be one of them. I'll show them what side I'm on before it comes to that."

"That's not the point."

"For the love of God, René, what is?"

He decided to say it straight out. "The villa. The prisoners of war. The internees. Orders will be clear: to wipe out every trace of the terrible things they've done in exchange for a lighter sentence.

He saw the color drain completely out of Simone's face as he digested what René was saying. "You're saying, with the enemy at their door, they'll order a complete whitewash." He needed to articulate the concept in order to assimilate it. He suddenly saw the scene clearly: fellow soldiers forced to commit atrocities, from destroying documents to who knew what else? Simone was floored. "How can they possibly erase something like this camp?" he asked. But formulating the question had provided him with the answer. René could tell because he started blinking furiously and his breathing had become shallow. Finally, he leaped into action. "There's no time to lose."

René thought now was the time to double down. "If they

really do manage to liberate Rome, it will already be too late for the villa."

Simone paced up and down, as if he were about to wet himself. One word from René had been enough to put him into battle mode. "Something needs to be done," he said, over and over again without stopping. "Yes, something needs to be done."

Working Simone up into a lather was risky, but René kept thinking about Mosca's face in the throes of death. The caress of communicating with Anna through the ceiling had not been enough, because the more time that passed the worse the prisoners' conditions got. They were losing their value, like bait that wasn't being nibbled at. At least he had boots to fix, buckles to mend. How would Anna be required to pay her keep at the villa?

Simone didn't know it, but there was another reason why he'd been incited to look at the liberation of Rome in a different light: the snow had almost completely melted; a few sparse piles resisted on the edge of the woods but green buds were bursting everywhere else.

René tried to explain that he had been forthright for the young soldier's sake not for his own. After all, prisoners would be protected on the chessboard of a liberated Italy, if they weren't "disappeared" first by Ciavatti or one of his henchmen, that is. Simone was in a different position. "It won't be enough to raise your hands and yell, 'I'm on your side even though I'm wearing the wrong uniform!'" Defecting to the other side required an action, something that would distinguish him beyond a shadow of a doubt. Ideally, an action that might be applauded.

Needless to say, Simone nodded furiously. Finally, he spoke up, no longer even listening to René's efforts to coax him in a certain direction. He uttered the words as if he were swearing before God. "All I know is that I'm ready to hand the keys of the villa over to the Allies, with the Germans hanging from hooks like legs of ham."

7

Anyone would think, listening to Simone, that liberating the wing of the seminary dedicated to political prisoners was the easiest thing in the world. The keys to the room were kept on a hook by the main door since none of the soldiers wanted the responsibility of looking after a set of keys that might get lost.

The rules were different for the other internees who divided their time between the common room and their dormitories. There would have been enough men among them to overcome the guards, but they had no weapons. A spray of a machine gun would soon derail their efforts. If a revolt were ever successful, there would be the sentry towers and barbed wire outside to get past.

At night, René would repeat all this information in a whisper. He would will his words up through the ceiling so that Anna could hear them. *Knock knock* . . . he told her that Simone had started secretly bringing him extra rations, though it wasn't a good idea to overdo it. If he didn't keep up that haggard look, the Nazi who came into the cell with his wash bowl every morning would soon realize his prisoner was fleshing out.

Simone would never think of precautions like this. He was on a different plane: he would formulate one wacky plan after another, as if he were chasing butterflies in a field. For a few days he'd been gripped by the idea of giving the whole contingent a sleeping potion, but had no idea where he would get hold of the drugs. The idea that he might be the one to open the gate to

Boscaglia and his band of partisans puffed him up to the eyeballs with pride.

The bishop was another matter. On signing the contract after the bombing of Grosseto, he had escaped the chaos of the burned-out city and its displaced citizens and moved into the villa. The Monsignor spent most of his time reading in his gilded rooms on the ground floor, or taking deathly slow walks in the gardens of the villa. Since the guests who were locked up on his premises were devotees of a different religion, the bishop never said mass, though he did offer them a Christmas and Epiphany lunch. His Eminence was taken care of by Sister Francesca, who was virtually invisible, and the two little priests-in-training who also lived there holed up like rats. Every now and again, the bishop would appear in the common room, bringing with him the aura of a saint. He would deign to mingle with the poor wretches and listen to their problems. Simone described the bishop as imperturbable; a man whose every gesture was calculated and who smiled all the time. "He doesn't look at things; he blesses them." Even the Nazi in command, who was apparently highly devoted to Christ, had been struck by the bishop's demeanor.

Monsignor Galeazzi loomed over the proceedings: he was there and not there, wafting through the villa like a bad smell, without ever interfering in the soldiers' work. It was disrupting to have a major player like the bishop around, a direct intermediary of God no less. Some of the prisoners read it as a sign of closeness and comfort; others felt the kiss of death. There was no doubt: this character would not have baulked at signing a rental contract with the governor of the province, knowing full well that the villa would be used to lock up families.

Another version—that the Monsignor had no choice—also did the rounds. Whatever the terms of the contract were, people said, his only option had been to give in to Ercolani's request.

If he had refused, the governor would have had no hesitation in using his iron fist to requisition the villa. If that had happened, the Monsignor would have been entirely cut off from the goings-on there. "There are families who are grateful to the bishop," Simone would say. "Mostly the ones who came to the prison camp of their own accord." They had seen it as a safe place to wait out the war, and it had come back to haunt them.

As Simone was telling René about the mess food, he was overwhelmed by a fit of yawning so extreme that it seemed like he wanted to swallow his own head. He was complaining about having to take turns in the bathroom to wash, and about drill practice; before going to bed he would write home but then he would forget to send his letters so they were piling up. In short, he was recounting the saga of life in the garrison, under the dark pall that had been hanging over them recently: the Blackshirts were nervous and the faces of the Maremma contingent of soldiers who were rethinking their strategy were as long as donkeys'. The more Simone talked, the more he felt trapped in a place where his talents were being wasted. "I feel like I'm floating in a dream," he would say. He hardly ever slept and, apparently, his thoughts had not been the only thing keeping him awake. There was a little girl among the prisoners who would keep the whole ground floor awake past midnight. The child had become obsessed with ghosts and there had been no way to calm her down, which meant Simone had been losing sleep, too. Rubbing his face with both hands, he would say "I open my eyes in the morning and I have no idea where I am. Then I feel a punch in the gut: I'm still locked up with the enemy, and they think I am fighting on their side."

René had Passini's boot on his lap, which to all intents and purposes looked like new. He placed it on the table and sat there for a while, contemplating his work. Then he said, "Tell me about this little girl."

Simone looked almost offended. René had never opened his

mouth to comment on any of his myriad plans and now he was asking for news of a kid with nightmares? Was he missing a cog? He said, "What do you mean?"

"Who is she? What does she do that keeps you up all night?"

"I don't know . . . She yells, she cries . . . René, is it so important?"

"Is she here with her parents?"

"I think so."

"What's her name?"

"René, how am I supposed to know? She's a kid, that's all I know."

"What does she say while she's having her nightmare?"

Simone felt his head was about to roll off with boredom. He really didn't want to waste another word on the subject: there was a war to fight. He shrugged. "I already told you; she's fixated with this ghost. She sees it standing at the end of her dormitory, or God know where else. But it's just the patrols going by."

"How do the soldiers react?"

"Nothing much happens. Her shrieks are agony for them, too. When it happens, they just hope she'll go back to sleep again as soon as possible." At this point he was well and truly fed up. He gave René a pat on the knee and jumped to his feet. "It's time, René. Time to close up shop. Yet another day and nothing to show for it."

When he saw the cobbler was smiling, the young soldier felt like he'd been shoved in the back.

8

It had been a perfectly normal night. Four prisoners had gone off the deep end, without the ghosts: eyes rolling back into their heads, convulsions, moans, and meaningless yelling; men who suddenly started beating themselves up; women whose hands had to be pinned to stop them ripping their own hair out. The lights in the dormitory had already been switched on, which had placated the anxious little girl obsessed with the ghost. But worse things were taking place in other parts of the dormitory.

Sleeping soldiers, including Simone, scrambled from their cots to address the emergency. Simone found himself guarding the perimeter of the dormitory with other soldiers, making sure everyone stayed where they were supposed to be while the Germans lashed out at the internees who were causing trouble, but to no effect whatsoever. The whole Maremma contingent looked on without lifting a finger as prisoners thrashed around on their mattresses like landed fish. The din woke the nuns, who started crossing themselves furiously and chanting the Lord's Prayer when they saw what was going on.

It went on for ten minutes. Then, just as it had started, it stopped. The prisoners fell back asleep, to the last man, and the silence that washed over the witnesses had the effect of a mudslide. The truce didn't last long, however. A soldier had taken things into his own hands and shaken one of the women awake, who instinctively shielded her eyes from the bright light. As soon as she realized she was surrounded by soldiers, she snapped into a sitting position on the cot. "What's going on?" she asked, dreading the worst. She hadn't the foggiest idea what had happened to her. As far as she was concerned, she'd been dreaming she was back home in Acquapendente, and had been very happy about it.

Some said that a bug was going around the camp. Others were more precise, but only confided in the people they could trust. They believed it was a hex sent by Satan; there was no other explanation. What do you expect if you turn a bishop's residence into a detention center? Meanwhile, even more prisoners were afflicted. As night fell, the soldiers' peeled their ears. They heard the first whimpers. Then wails, and more cries. In no time at all, all hell broke loose, with almost all of the prisoners writhing on their beds, making the beds slam against one another. The soldiers looked on, horrified. A bedlam of shrieks, howls, arms reaching up towards the heavens as though their owners were being burned at the stake. The nuns at the door were on their knees, but their rosaries were not powerful enough to put an end to it. Whatever had possessed the dormitory was a superior force.

The worst part was when everything calmed down and went back to usual. There was darkness in the soldiers' eyes in the wake of the commotion: a combination of shock, terror, and guilt. Even the Nazis found it hard to get a hold of themselves: a monkey was sitting on their shoulder which, together with the news from the front, was enough to shrink their pupils to pin points. Bombs and rifle shots were one thing, but the invisible wind blowing over the villa was quite another. It kept coming and going. Like a warning. An exhortation. Once a week at least, the earth would open up under their feet and wails would rise from the circles of hell. Even when the noise stopped, it was hard to tuck the memory of it away somewhere; it would haunt them for the rest of the night, and creep into their dreams. The following morning, the soldiers would wake up with a heavy heart that would weigh them down for the rest of the day. Until the next time.

Since Monsignor Galeazzi wouldn't leave his rooms, they decided to call Dr. Salghini for a professional opinion. As soon as the commotion started, they sent for him posthaste and dragged him out of his bed. After a few minutes of mayhem, he asked for a chair and a shot of spirits. He was staggering, his eyes wandering everywhere but in the direction of the dormitory. At one point, he hung his head as if he were in the dock facing a mob of accusers. The sensation was spreading, as if, all of a sudden, the soldiers had become prisoners. On taking his leave, Dr. Salghini made his diagnosis: mass hysteria, he possessed no cure.

It was hard for the soldiers to accept that the bishop didn't stir even when through the gate came Don Lauro, an insignificant country priest . . . As embarrassed as the others were by the bishop's absence, Don Lauro's verdict was predictable: it was the devil at work. The German commanding officer was not amused. He was no fool and he could see both his soldiers and the Maremma contingent cowering in the corner. By the time the guards on night duty arrived at the sentry towers, their nerves were in tatters and they were in danger of opening fire on a stray cat coming out of the bushes.

It transpired that the prisoners would wake up feeling refreshed, while the soldiers were falling to pieces. All of a sudden, the soldiers started treating the families imprisoned in the villa more gently. The Blackshirts pretended to be hard-nosed, but they had lost their resolve. They kept their distance and left the dirty work to the others. Ciavatti could well have dealt with the matter with a simple order: shoot them all and throw them into a mass grave. The way things were heading, however, he would have struggled to find soldiers willing to execute the order. Wartime decree laws were one thing, but calling down a curse on them all was another.

Those who were not superstitious continued to talk about some kind of virus that attacked the nerves, which meant they were worse off than the others, testing their food and drink one drop at a time. A request for a supply of gas masks to be brought to the villa had also been sent in. How could anyone be sure this was not an attack? Were they certain that the epidemic didn't come from the water they drank at table, or washed in? Were the communists to blame? Were Allied forces sabotaging them from behind the lines?

Whatever the explanation, the rampant sickness in the bishop's villa was clearly evidence that evil was being perpetrated there. It had become more than a suspicion for those already inclined to think in those terms. It started to change the minds of the firmest supporters of the regime.

Bedtime in the dormitory had become a ritual that sent shivers down everyone's spines. As soon as the lights went out, the prisoners' breathing patterns started to change. Two hours later, the first gasp arrived. A moan answered from the other side of the large room. A wheeze. A creaking of bedsprings. Until the floor started to shake, sounding like a hundred drums rolling. And all hell let loose. The first shriek was a talon scratching the soldiers' faces; some would instinctively take a step back. In that moment, the message was palpable: a child had seen a ghost, and now the whole dormitory was possessed, which meant it was not entirely unlikely that a gaping hole would open in the floor, and flames would start licking the ceiling. Or nothing would happen and that was perhaps worse. Waiting for something that failed to materialize was even more exhausting.

The inmates in the dormitory were giving voice to the many ghosts they carried inside them, ghosts that everyone collects during a war. Including the Nazis, who appeared unable to get used to those satanic shouting matches. Who knows what they thought when one of their own crumpled onto his knees? In the middle of that macabre dance, in fact, a big Nazi oaf had collapsed right in front of all those possessed souls. In a fit of hysterics, he writhed and kicked just like the prisoners, making the room reverberate. The other German guards stripped him of his weapon and stood there with bated breath, staring at their slack-jawed, cross-eyed fellow soldier.

It was true, then. No one had been spared. The soldiers were beginning to catch the disease, too. A stretcher was brought in and the big Nazi was taken to the infirmary. When he woke up, he looked around for a while and spoke German, although he might as well have been speaking Italian because everyone in the room understood what he was saying. From his expression, it was clear that he didn't remember a thing. He was taking stock of things as if he'd had a terrible hangover. Eventually, he came to his senses and started wailing that he'd caught the infection. Or that the devil had taken him. There was no point in telling him it was a nervous breakdown. There were cases of mass hysteria every day in war: all it took was one soldier to cough, and all the others would follow suit. One soldier happened to have an irremediable case of nausea or dizziness, and the same afternoon the whole unit needed a vacation in the rearguard. The same mechanism applied there at the villa: the fits had spread from one child to the whole dormitory. And from there to the Germans.

Ciavatti's appearance on the scene made things worse. Exhausted by the constant laments, he came from the garrison to see what was going on with his own eyes. To begin with, his arrival gave the Maremma soldiers a little courage. Every one of them was anxious to demonstrate the witchcraft to the Maresciallo's deputy. When the shrieking was at its worst, the officer reached for his holster. He took out his gun and shot into the air. The bullet lodged in the ceiling, but the howling went on. He may have been tempted to take aim at a random bed and try again—how would the prisoners react if they'd been pretending?—but it would have been a crazy move. The nerves of the whole battalion were hanging on a spider's thread: murdering someone possessed by the devil in cold blood would be inhuman, and would spell doom for everyone present. Accordingly, Ciavatti strode off, and struck the first man to cross his path with his baton. Twice on the legs. The prisoner stopped yelling, and shook himself out of the curse, only to find himself with a smashed shinbone. The officer grinned at his men. "You see? You just need to wake them up." The soldiers responded ashen-faced, as if they had taken the beating personally. In any case, nobody took his advice. It was better to ride the wave of madness, which only ever lasted up to fifteen minutes, than endure a hundred or so prisoners screaming blue murder day and night over their broken bones.

René didn't see any great changes from his room, with the exception of the German guard who now no longer spat in his bowl in the mornings, but hung his head without saying a word. He wouldn't even look at the prisoner; he would take the few steps from the door to the table and then turn on his heels and leave. Simone would arrive soon after with the sacks and they would set up the work table. The young soldier had revived recently, and didn't seem to suffer as much when he told René stories about life in the camp. He would sometimes have so much to say that the torrent of words turned back on themselves, forming a dam, and he would just stand there gasping, his mouth hanging open like a fish. His eyes wide open, he would murmur, "René!" Like a child unable to describe a treasure they'd chanced upon under a stone.

9.

He wrapped the front tail of his shirt around the handle to muffle any creaking. When the door opened, he felt the air shift.

It hadn't been difficult for Simone to pretend he had been closing it behind him: it took two turns of the key to close and two to open it. "We just have to hope nobody comes by to check," the young soldier had said. Which had never actually happened, even before the evil spell; now, the wing devoted to political prisoners was practically unguarded after nightfall.

There was one long corridor running along the first and second floors, without any turns leading anywhere else, and only one set of stairs to get up or down. The windows were all barred. Naturally, the two soldiers on guard duty kept each other company on the ground floor. At least they had someone to talk to. To kill time with. And anyway, since the sickness had set in, there was no way the guards weren't sticking together. They spent their whole shift downstairs, as close as possible to the bishop's quarters. Simone knew this.

In fact, when René left his room, there was no one around, only the searchlights washing over him. From one second to the next, he found himself walking barefoot along the corridor, opening doors to rooms he knew were empty and leaving them wide open. He had been well trained. He would be able to draw a map of the whole villa and mark those holding prisoners with an X.

And the prisoners were the problem. As soon as he fished

the keys off the hook and put them in the lock, he could hear shuffling sounds from inside. He went over what Simone had told him. "They're reduced to skin and bones; they're kept like that on purpose. Even if they get the chance, they won't be able to take more than three steps to escape. It's unlikely they'll approach you, but you never know."

Carrying a knife with the idea you may need to use it on someone is a very different matter from having one with you for the sake of it. Simone had chosen the biggest one in René's bag of tools and handed it to him. "You need to keep them against the wall. They may see the door open, and realize you're not a guard. They could go crazy and rush for the exit like drunk animals."

As he entered the first door, René came out with the stupidest phrase possible. In a wispy voice, he said, "May I come in?"

He knew there were two of them in there, and spotted them right away. They were curled up in a ball, each in their own corner. The smell embarrassed him. Did Simone experience the same stench when he came into his own cell? Holding the knife down by his side, he said, "I'm here to free you, but not right now."

He wouldn't have bet a toe-nail on it, but keeping the political prisoners under control was easier than he had expected. As that mass of demoniacs was making the dormitory quake below, René calmly explained his reason for paying a night visit to those huddled men, who looked so poorly they wouldn't have been able to reach the toilet bucket to spit in. They hardly said a word, hardly grunted a response. The few words he did hear after telling his little tale were delirious and he was able to make out a nod of agreement in only a very few cases. One inmate started sobbing. "What day is it today? Has Rachel turned twelve yet or not?"

He went from room to room bringing tidings of a particular kind of revolt that required no action whatsoever. All the prisoners had to do was stay exactly where they were and ignore the fact that the door had been left open. They weren't to worry; they would soon be getting out. Just not that night. If they wanted the villa to be brought down, they mustn't move. They were going to gnaw at the seminary from the inside, like clothes moths. His most important recommendation was that nobody should ever mention they had laid eyes on him. On his way out, he hung each key back on its hook.

After leaving open the doors to parlors and fetid rooms, he went up a flight of stairs to the floor above. Standing in front of the door he thought must be Anna's, his hands were shaking so badly that it took the strength of a Titan to turn the key.

On his right, he saw the imposing outline of a very big man leaning against the wall with his elbows on his knees. Anna was curled up asleep under the window. They had given her a heavy jacket to put on, but the long hair splayed out on the floor was a giveaway.

"Anna," he gasped, his heart hammering in his chest. "Anna, it's me . . . "

Keeping an eye on the colossus, he whispered, "Anna, wake up. Can you hear me?"

"I know you," the man said, getting immediately to his feet. He slid along the wall, using it for support. "Maciste, is that you?"

He couldn't see the face, but the man's voice and stature conjured up the image of the young giant who had been in Anna's apartment with Mosca after Faina had knocked him out.

The man pulled himself up to his full height. It was clear from the limp that his right leg had been damaged. "Is Boscaglia here? I knew he wouldn't abandon us."

No, Boscaglia was not there. René was not proposing an escape, but he did have a plan that required the mastodon to get back down again pronto. He went straight to the point. "What's wrong with Anna? Why isn't she waking up?" Without waiting for an answer, he swept into the room and leaned over the woman just as the behemoth said, "What do you mean? She's not . . . " René bent down and gently turned her over. The man went on, "She's running a fever. Her name is Maria. They captured us in the farmhouse."

With another woman's face, Anna's eyelids fluttered and, clearing her throat, she murmured, "Damiano . . . " René brushed the hair off her forehead. She was burning alive. "Damiano, take me home. I'm so tired . . . " she said, smiling. Then she fell asleep on the spot.

"Are you the one knocking on the ceiling?" the big man asked.

René was bereft of all desire. The giant would have to be satisfied with the explanations he had already given. He watched René leave the room, barefoot, treading like a sleep-walker, the knife dangling from his good hand.

He dragged his way back down the corridor, past wide-open rooms, feeling hollowed out, and didn't even turn around when he heard a voice call out to him, "Hey, you—?" Finally, he crept back into his cell and hunkered down into a corner. He didn't move an inch until the following morning, when the alarm was raised.

The first soldiers to respond didn't even check whether the prisoners were still in their cells: on glimpsing the wide-open doors they had simply run. Boot heels clattered on all sides, making the floor shake. Incomprehensible commands flew this way and that, sounding very much like cries for help from under enemy fire. Then the discovery, which was perhaps even more shocking than if there'd been a great escape, that everyone had been accounted for. By all accounts, the prisoners had woken up to the surprise. After a string of bedeviled nights, the message that had started to take shape in the guards' minds was loud and clear: the situation had nothing to do with bacteria. The villa itself was willing the prisoners to be freed.

Having set up his work table, René threw the knife back into the pile with his other tools. When Simone found out about Rizziello's little ploy, he said, "What a bastard," and went on to relate how soldiers who had seen the war from up close all of a sudden had to make a supreme effort just to get past the villa gates.

René wasn't listening: from the get-go, the Maresciallo had made him believe the woman who had been arrested was Anna. It had been a way to get him to talk, in case he'd had anything to say. After being locked up for all that time, after the beatings, he'd discovered it had never been true.

10

S imone asked René repeatedly how come there'd been no trace of Alfredo up there on the second floor. He'd formed an attachment to the young partisan. It hadn't simply been a matter of friendship; it was also a badge of honor. Alberto would be able to tell the world the real role Simone had played in the war. The idea of losing a witness as valuable as Alberto drove him to distraction.

In the end, they always left the subject hanging there, since neither of them could face speculating about how Rizziello and Ciavatti had rid themselves of that particular prisoner.

René thought about the young giant, Maciste, who he now knew was being held prisoner as well. If he decided to be a total jerk, there were two possible outcomes. The first: here come the Nazis, who, having found out about his nocturnal stroll, would break his bones. The second involved a more subtle reaction and concerned Simone, the only soldier in the whole camp who had dealings with René. The only one who could have helped him get out of his cell.

Still reeling from the betrayal of discovering there was no friend in the camp to save, René had lost all his verve. He watched events unfold like a snake eating its tail. The frightened René came back to the fore: what had been the point of his great act of courage? The first and only one in his life, he realized. The only outcome was that he'd ended up in prison behaving like a fool, tied to the apron-strings of a ghost. He had sacrificed everything for a giant blunder, and now he didn't even have the energy to lick his wounds.

All the while, the possessed continued their evening concert. Simone was concerned that, after the little matter of the wide-open doors, the soldiers would be getting used to all the weird things going on at the villa. "There's one more thing," he announced one morning. "Galeazzi has started visiting the internees again." The Monsignor had stayed longer than strictly necessary. Simone told him the bishop had called some of the men over and engaged in deep conversation with them.

A few days later, Ercolani gave the order to transfer a number of families.

"The list is ready." Simone didn't know yet whether to consider this good news or bad. "Those with surnames from A-M will be going."

René was hammering a nail into the heel of a boot, mostly to keep him busy rather than because he was required to. "Where are they taking them?"

"Up to Emilia. There's a collection camp there. They say they'll be transported to Germany from there."

"What for?"

"I don't know. Nobody knows. Not even Rizziello."

He thought maybe there were villas like this one in Germany, or prisons. The fact of the matter was that being transported up to northern Italy just as the Allies were heading for Rome was bad luck.

Simone grinned, with a sudden cunning look. "There's more news, René." The young soldier glanced over at the corridor then said, "The bus parked in front of the camp for the past two days has not gone unnoticed by the partisans. They've heard something is going to happen soon."

"How do you know?"

"There are tracks around the villa, which means they are here. Maybe they never left. The Maresciallo is going crazy."

Two families who had seemingly benefited from the bishop's

protection had been taken off the transport list. A sick note had been sufficient. If the rumors Simone had heard were to be believed, exempting a protected circle from the transfer didn't bode well. Why not just let them go to the transit camp with the others? The governor of the province must be feeling the Allies breathing down his neck and the decision to transport the prisoners up north was his attempt to sweep all the dirt under the carpet. There was no other explanation.

The inmates at the villa were not stupid, however. With the upcoming transport in mind, they rattled the cots in the dormitory as if to send a clear message to the bishop, soldiers, and nuns. Worse: fathers and husbands were trying to make contact any way they could. They wanted concrete information about why, how, and when the families would be moved, and whether there really was a plan for an escape.

In no time at all, a war-within-the-war had broken out between the families who had friends in high places and those who didn't have a saint in heaven to appeal to. Fights were more frequent than ever, and the Germans made everyone pay the consequences. Their discomfort was a hungry beast, filling its stomach minute by minute. They had plenty of worries to nourish it, what with the night curse, the Allies' advance, the partisans' tracks deliberately provoking them, and the planned transport. In the middle of this earthquake, there was Simone, who risked being outed at any moment. In fact, he stayed away from the common room, which, in its turn, made the prisoners even more unhappy, as the only friendly face they had left appeared to have abandoned them.

The night-patrol shift was doubled. One morning, Simone told René, a young soldier had come down, his face still scrunched up with sleep. He said he'd seen something. "There was one of those little priests who hang out with the bishop. I saw him out of the corner of my eye under the searchlight."

"What was he doing?"

"It was a matter of seconds, but I'd bet my life on it. I saw him throwing something out of the window."

"What was it?"

"Who knows? I didn't even hear it land. He must have wrapped whatever it was in a cloth."

Nobody could tell whether the war of conscience that had been raging in the dormitory had seeped through the walls and whetted the bishop's curiosity. A whiff of the Allies' imminent presence, confirmed by plans for the upcoming prisoner transport, could have been further encouragement. Torn between ghouls inside the villa and ghosts outside, Monsignor Galeazzi had clearly decided to make a move, leaving the cobbler and the young soldier shocked by the news that he may well already have been in contact with the partisans.

11

O n the day of the transport, René gazed out of his window at the Spring. There were leafy woods and an echoing soundtrack of rumbling engines and barked orders. When René saw that Simone was late, he assumed he was involved in the upheavals of that exceptional morning. He pictured the families, the confused kids after months in the villa being herded onto a bus and taken who knows where.

Every now and again he found himself thinking about what would happen to the prisoners in his wing when the powers that be decided to make them disappear. He dwelt on the question, as if he were testing himself for a reaction. But he felt nothing. Being incarcerated had changed his view of himself, and watching events unfold made him feel like someone other than himself who was leaning on a windowsill and looking out on another world. At another time. The revelation of Anna's absence had been the final blow. He thought back to the moment when he'd turned the woman's body over. He could hear the guffaws of his drinking buddies at the Due Porte rising up from deep inside him.

His heart started racing when he realized that Simone was not coming. He pressed his ear to the window, but he could no longer hear yells or engines revving in front of the villa. The notion that the young soldier had been arrested and locked up somewhere thanks to the giant snitch upstairs almost made his knees buckle. As the minutes passed, René started talking to his young friend. "What have they done to you?" The cell was shrinking around him and his breath was turning into lime dust. He was so exasperated that he started thumping on the door, the thuds echoing grimly. "Guard! Guard!" he yelled, but there was no response. He paced the perimeter of his cell like a madman, for miles and miles.

He asked the soldier who finally brought in his lunch rations. "Is the workshop closed today?" No answer.

No sir, I'm not losing another son, he swore to himself, gritting his teeth. The only response was an expanse of thick wall, a lock with four turns of the key, and bars at the window. "Guard!" He shredded his throat yelling at the top of his voice, as if it was the first time he realized he was incarcerated. Meanwhile, the day grew darker and the shadows closed in, as if to confirm that he was doomed. By the time his evening meal was brought in, he still hadn't touched his lunch. The soldier on guard duty barely noticed. He picked up the tray, under the steady gaze of the German standing at the door as usual. "Why haven't you brought my tools?" he said. The German barked something back. As soon as the Maremma soldier was close enough, however, he couldn't help whispering, "Where is Simone?" The German caught wind of their attempt to communicate and rushed in with his rifle cocked. Standing in front of the cobbler, he turned the weapon around, as if he were about to hit him with the butt. René looked the officer in the eye. In the end, the German ordered his Italian underling to desist, and they both went out.

The night swept away every doubt: he would never see Simone again. The big blabber-mouth upstairs must have given the authorities everything they needed and he imagined Simone at Ciavatti's mercy. He also thought about Alfredo and all the other prisoners of war locked up in that wing of the seminary being turned into silent screams. All of a sudden, he decided he would give them a voice.

He started softly, producing the yelps of a nervous dog. He

had to gain confidence in his throat, which was producing a rough paste after months of hardly opening his mouth, or at most whispering. When he tried to fill his lungs, he was convulsed by coughs. But he didn't give up. Rather, he doubled his efforts. The timbre of his voice was infernal. He kicked the chair against the door, making more din than an entire army. Then he started letting rip for real.

While catching his breath he listened attentively. On his night escapade, he'd encountered human wrecks, men on their last legs, so he didn't have high hopes. Most of them probably didn't even remember they had received an apparition that night.

He was almost overwhelmed by a wave of emotion when he heard a voice coming from someplace, as if it had simply seeped through the walls. Another voice came from closer by. Coughing. Banging. First cautious, then louder and louder. It was like blowing on a fire that was threatening to die out at any moment. Drunk with rage at the thought of Simone, René roared with all his strength. He was whipping up mayhem. Hearing his howls, more and more decrepit wolves were encouraged to join the pack and bay with him in chorus.

He wondered how the big traitor was taking it. Could he hear their hollering? They were the cries of people he had betrayed and he would take their laments with him to the grave. And was the bishop down there feeling the weight of that cherub-frescoed ceiling crush his chest after being woken up by yet another diabolical ruckus?

His door was suddenly thrown open. They found René on the floor, as if he were rolling in flames. He was prepared for a beating, but all it would do was feed his desperation. They didn't dare touch him and locked him back up.

By the time he stopped yelling, he was no more than an empty sack. His bloodied wounds were itching from head to toe. An immense wave of fatigue washed over him and he listened to it as it invaded his bones. Without the lead voice, the rest of them started to quiet down, relaxing into a kind of lullaby. As silence reclaimed its place in that wing of the seminary, his eyelids grew heavier and heavier until he fell into a deep sleep without even noticing.

12

By the time the door opened again, René had already made up his mind: he would never speak nor eat again. Let them skin him alive. That fruitless revolution be damned; he couldn't care less anymore.

Simone appeared on the threshold with the usual sack of boots. "Good morning," he said brightly, plonking the sack on the table. The cobbler looked at him with a dazed expression, as if he were looking at an actual ghost. He watched the young soldier as he retrieved his work tools. "Things were a bit tense last night, I heard."

So, Simone's cover hadn't been blown. Rather, he'd been assigned to the prison transport detail to Livorno. The convoy was then handed over to another squadron for the following leg to Romagna. "I was in the army van tailing the bus," Simone went on. "There was another one in front."

The journey had been uneventful, especially once they had driven down the mountain and reached the coast. There had been just one moment when Simone had been scared to death: almost at the beginning of their journey, on one of the hairpin bends before getting to Montemassi, with the outline of Le Case silhouetted up there on the peak in full view, like a picture postcard. "There was some kind of failure. They had us all get out at rifle point."

"What kind of failure?"

"That's what the driver called it. He suddenly pulled over to check the brakes. The other soldiers were taking it easy, enjoying the sun. I couldn't get that little trainee priest at the sentry tower out of my head. I was the only one to know that the failure may have been part of a plan to ambush us. I kept my eye on the two Nazis in command. I would have gunned them down without batting an eye as soon as I heard the first shot. After that, they could do with me what they wanted, but there was no way I was going to die a Fascist."

Simone sounded almost apathetic as he said this. René thought that he, too, must have lost his sense of self-preservation. The war and the villa had changed them both to the point that the idea of dying no longer scared either of them.

"But the partisans didn't show up?"

"Maybe the message the priest threw out of the window got there too late. It might still be there. Or who knows what happened? The fact is, we set off again, as if we were on vacation. When I saw the sea, I started to cry. Imagine."

"So, was there a failure?"

Simone sighed. "What do you think?"

He didn't believe there had been. A hitch like that on the first prisoner transport was more than a coincidence. The Germans were not born yesterday. "That driver took a risk," René said. "Do we know who he is?"

Simone had kept his eye on him as the families had been moved from the first bus to the next, and then again on their return, when he sat with another soldier on the same bus he'd been driving before. He was beefy and cantankerous, with big workman's hands. He didn't say a word the whole journey. All he did for practically the whole trip was whistle—tunes with no rhyme or reason that he probably invented as he went along. "At the end of the trip, they handed him his wages as if he had just dumped a load of muck for them. Then he left."

The internees were unsettled. From one day to the next, twenty-one people were missing from roll call. Those who had been removed from the transport list found themselves unable to rejoice. Bishop's favorites or not, they were disturbed by the unoccupied beds in the dormitory. The vacant spaces wailed more desperately than writhing bodies.

Evidently, Hercules upstairs had not gabbed. Moreover, the bishop had been in contact with the partisans: organizing an ambush would be within his divine remit, after all. Or else, the trainee priest was the one juggling all the balls, leaving His Eminence out of it. Finally, there had been mayhem again that night, which Simone said had adversely affected the Maremma contingent in the seminary: they saw it as an umpteenth reproach from God after the families had been taken away. The supernatural phenomena going on in the wing housing the internees gave everyone goosebumps. Political prisoners, like René, had no idea what kind of devilish disease had possessed the dormitory. "Some soldiers feel like they have the blood of Jesus on their hands," Simone said. "René, find me a pope who would disagree."

In any case, there was no doubt in his mind that it had started: Ercolani was beginning to clean up. This meant that the stench of the Allies was already wafting towards Grosseto, and that the Fascists could smell it as far inland as Le Case. The haunted prisoner strategy was slowly eroding the Nazi's nerves. It may even have pricked the bishop's conscience. The only problem was that the villa was now more heavily guarded than ever.

13

He was on the brink of sleep when he heard steps coming to the door, and then the rattling of keys. They pointed a flashlight at him. "On your feet."

"What—?" he started to say, but they had already grabbed him and were dragging him out of the room.

They made their way along the corridor at speed. Soldiers were imparting orders in hushed tones. It felt like they were on a secret mission.

Stepping out into the open made him almost pass out: after weeks locked inside, the star-filled sky seemed to be sucking him in. But there was no time to lose. "Move, move!" Other prisoners, weakened by starvation, were collapsing around him, only to be picked up by strong arms on both sides and pulled along, their knees dragging on the grass.

René looked back at the villa. All the lights were out. His only landmarks were the searchlights on the sentry towers, which sliced the woods in two rather than beaming their light on the commotion that was taking place around him. They came to a halt in front of the open door of an army van. "Get in," the soldier on his right said. Another gave him a shove from behind. He climbed in.

There were other people inside. "What's going on?" he asked. "Where are they taking us?" Nobody answered. A young prisoner in front of him was bawling his eyes out. René looked out. It was impossible to distinguish the faces of the soldiers involved in the operation; all he could see were their outlines.

He couldn't even identify their uniforms. Another prisoner was thrown on board, landing practically on top of him. Then another. They slammed the door shut. Someone thumped the side of the van twice, and they were off.

The evacuation was so quick that anyone would think the bishop's villa was on fire. Yet, it was still standing there, frozen, watching the scene with a hundred shadowy eyes. The van was being driven nervously; on every curve they were pitched from side to side like sacks of potatoes. There was another behind them, its headlights intermittently illuminating the haggard faces around him. There must have been at least ten of them. Piled in. Their heads crashing into one another like billiards at every unforeseen turn. Then the surface of the road changed and there were no more ruts. The rumbling of the wheels on the tarmac blended with the roar of the engine. Someone started coughing. Another said, "Is this how we'll end our days?" The young prisoner in front of him leaned forward and retched. He wept and spat, and then tried to catch his breath, but it sounded as if he couldn't get air back into his lungs. A badly-navigated bend sent them all lurching to the left. A second later, another curve had them careening the other way. René felt an elbow or something else strike his forehead and he sat there in a daze, with something warm trickling down his face. The sounds and lights from the van behind them were fading; everything was as muffled as if a bell jar had been placed over his head. When they swerved again, he was thrust inertly into the mix, too feeble to soften the impact with his arms.

In the Thick

1.

Snatching at flashes of a dream: a shadow, rustling, words that sounded back to front. The effort of understanding what was going on, of trying to move, catapulted him back into the darkness. But he resisted, opening his eyes instead. Every time he did so, the light was different. Or there was a sudden blast of heat and the stench of kerosene. His mind was at a standstill, and he wasn't even sure whether he was in possession of a body.

Little by little, he began to conquer the waves of drowsiness. His wakeful moments grew longer and he was able to take in new details. René was beholding the world as an amazed and uncomprehending newborn baby would: a color, a breath of air, a sound . . . sometimes a touch. He could feel a damp cloth on his forehead and so he gave it a name: "water." Then, "thirst." Followed by "well," "river," "rain" . . . a bucket with spit in it, sabers of light slashing through the night. *Knock, knock.* The face of a woman who was not who he thought.

Rambling recapitulations observed from an unfamiliar place. Soft bread was brought to his mouth, and he ate it. Hunger, dinners by the fireplace, letters burned in the fire . . . Whenever he slipped back into darkness, the images would return; opening his eyes again, a tiny detail was enough to conjure up scenes from recent and distant times that gushed out of the depths of his being, like the echoes of old songs. His first nickname, Pistola, the kisses Dora Palmieri denied him, a blood-soaked lathe, a young soldier asking whether local chicks swallowed cock chowder . . .

They pulled him up into a sitting position, but he was still unable to speak. It was Tormenta, the one with a brigand's moustache, who came and cleaned him, turning him as if he were as light as a feather. Wiping his ass, he would always say, "Maciste, it would be fine if you shat less, God bless you." Then he would give him a sip of spirits from the hip flask he kept in his coat pocket. "Have a drop of antibiotic," he would mutter. One day, René almost made him drop it in shock when he said, "More."

The strands he was beginning to weave together brought whole sequences of his life back to the fore, and he would contemplate them for afternoons at a time. There were some giant gaps, however, that made it hard for him to know who he was. The edges were so faded he wasn't even sure which facts belonged to him. There was also the matter of the name they were calling him by. "Maciste" didn't mean much to him. Every now and again, he would ask Tormenta, trying out words and surprising himself with his own voice. "Who am I, for real?" Tormenta would stare at him, twirling a little stick he would always be chewing on to make his cigarettes last longer. "You're Maciste." And he would explain the whole thing to him all over again. That where he was now, every combatant was either given a battle name or chose one for themselves. It was a way to protect both the brigade and their families. If a partisan was captured, it was hard for the Germans to glean the kind of details that would send them straight to their family homes to surprise their wives, children, or parents. Nobody in the woods kept documents in their bags, that was for sure. Of course, a hostage may be in the area, and in that case, everything depended on their ability to withstand the beatings. The best thing was to send locals away to another brigade, far away from home. Two towns away, where they would be as good as foreign, was usually enough. It wasn't always possible, however, and it could even backfire: in war, close knowledge of an area was often crucial.

Tormenta never went out with the group that left the hide-out in the morning. At first, René thought he stayed back to take care of him. It was only once they'd started talking that he realized he hadn't been out for months on end, so many that he had stopped counting. He was too old for incursions, so he'd taken guard duty. If he spotted anything untoward, he'd been instructed to set in motion a series of actions, such as running to various spots and throwing stones, or breaking certain branches, etcetera, so that the partisans would immediately be alerted if anything was amiss as they made their way back to their base.

After spending so long in the woods, Tormenta had started to talk to himself. Dealing with the endless snow storms had been an adventure he would only have wished on the Nazis, though it gave him his battle name, which meant "blizzard." He'd been cut off by the snow for weeks, his rations running dangerously low. In that sea of solitude, there'd come a time when words in his head or uttered out loud had ceased to have any meaning. Tormenta had been truly terrified. During those candlelit nights, he used to recite the names of his extended family, to make sure he wouldn't forget them, or, more impor-tantly, himself. He would associate a scene with every name. "Uncle Valente—that time when he gave me a glass of wine aged five and made me pass out. My mom beat him with her broomstick for it; Amanda, my ugly, dumb cousin—that time she convinced me at sixteen to give her a kiss down there. She gave me a book in exchange for doing her the service, which I never read, and now I wish I had it here to keep me com-pany; Dad—forget him; Nonna Francesca—today I went and picked a flower for her." When the band had finally managed to get back to their hideout, they'd found him with a long beard at the end of the cave. The first thing Tormenta had said was, "When I speak, can you hear me or am I talking to myself?" His fellow partisans had been tipped off to his mental condition right away. One of them was quick-witted enough to say, "Hey, have you lost your tongue? Come on, say something!" A second later, they were all over him and managed to grab the knife he was about to use to slice his own throat.

There were three other partisans in the band. They would come back as soon as dusk started to fall. They would bring news and sacks filled with supplies that Tormenta put away before cooking dinner. They were all young men; not a day over thirty. They would talk about certain operations, or comment on rumors they had gathered. They never asked after René, nor did they waste their energy greeting him. A nod of the head, maybe, or a glance to check on his condition. For all he knew, they considered him a parasite, eating their potatoes without having earned them. His presence helped soothe the nerves of their comrade, who had had more than enough of being left behind on his own, and that was at least one thing he had going for him. When they recounted their day, they would form a huddle and start whispering, shoulder to shoulder.

René didn't know their battle names. Tormenta had been careful never to talk about them when they were out. They made him feel like an enemy who didn't need to be chained up because his broken leg was holding him there. Alongside the terrible blow to the head that still made him nauseous if he so much as turned his head.

One day, Tormenta told him the story of how the cobbler had come to be in their midst. It sounded to René like one of those old legends, handed down by the fire from father to son. There was once an evil villa where they had jailed lots of families with the help of a bishop . . . When this reality returned to him in flashes it was like an earthquake striking; an invisible hand reached inside him, moving all the components around. The doors to rooms that had been closed with several turns of the key after the accident were all of a sudden unlocked; one door or another would open wide and he would find pieces of himself in there.

The strangest thing was finding himself being described by Tormenta as a prisoner. Neither Tormenta, nor the other lads who came back to the den in the evening had any idea what crime he had been accused of that merited his being locked up in a cell, but having found him together with the other exhausted prisoners had been a sufficient badge of honor. And there was more: after the ambush, after the shooting, after the prisoners had been freed, one of the partisans had recognized him. "Faina vouched for you. He said, 'That's Maciste' when he first looked inside the van."

It felt like there was a secret world bubbling up under him, and his task was to relieve the pressure in order to let out the truth. But the blockage was more like a brick wall, and he only had his fingernails to claw at it. After listening to the fairy tale about his liberation, he slept so soundly he almost entered another world. The man who had been guarding him had to slap his face to wake him. René opened his eyes, only to find Tormenta's big face in front of him. "None of that funny business, do you hear?" he said.

His leg was not doing well. Whenever it had to be cleaned and the splint re-set, he saw stars. Tormenta would prepare him with a few sips from his hipflask and then stick a belt between his teeth. Pulling the splint off, the loosening sent a jolt of pain through him that almost made him black out. "This isn't going back to normal. Come on, try and move it."

It was so agonizing that, like a child, he begged Tormenta not to do anything. He would be happy to keep his leg as it was, but there was no way his guardian would stop. "Maimed *and* crippled, Maciste? Is that how you want to end your days? Get on with it and stop bleating."

René convinced himself that Tormenta was getting a kick

out of torturing him. The man would goad him to the point that his pain would turn into a rush of sudden anger, together with an urge to kick his tormentor. Lifting his heel from the pallet, he would roar in agony. "Your knee is moving all wrong," Tormenta would comment, as if he were examining it for the first time. Seeing René done in with exertion, Tormenta would give in and hold the hipflask to his patient's mouth. "Here, drink," he would say, all the while watching the wreck of a man before him. He seemed to feed off the sight. Then he would put the splint back on and René would invariably pass out.

Tormenta might well have lost his marbles at some point, but there was no one else willing to spend their days at his sickbed. Another thing his guardian would always say when he was cleaning him was, "Maciste, if you ever find that you're stinking rich, don't forget what I did for you here."

Meanwhile, memories continued to strike him like little lightning bolts out of the blue: flashes of life in the cell, Simone slumped in the gilt-legged chair, even bursts of their conversations. He didn't talk about it. If anything, he carried on pretending to be as oblivious as ever. It was the only advantage he had. Soon he would be begging for mercy again, when his guardian decided it was time to take care of his leg. That was what he would say, "Maciste, it's time to take care of your leg." René would fold his hands in prayer and promise Tormenta everything under the sun, but it was no use: the man wasn't satisfied until he heard him yell.

2

The band would announce their return by imitating the cry of a curlew: three calls. Pause. Then, one. They would repeat the sequence until Tormenta responded with another sound, like the chirp of a sparrow. One evening, seven of them arrived.

The guardian of the den was having a field day, suddenly behaving like an old nonna surprised by a visit from her grandchildren. "Come in, come in," he said, kicking odds and ends to one side to make room. The guests didn't stand on ceremony. They threw their sacks down and lined up their rifles in a corner.

Under normal conditions, the cave was just big enough for the usual five; suddenly, it was like fitting a jigsaw puzzle together. They had brought two big bottles of wine, which they immediately started passing around. Tormenta, in the meantime, was already at work, opening packages and putting away supplies. The excitement at seeing new faces sent him into a state of child-like trepidation.

The new arrivals were just as young as the others; only one of them had a dash of salt and pepper in his sideburns. To make up for this, there was a tawny, pale, taciturn young man who lowered the average considerably—despite his weary air and dirty appearance after a long march, he could not have been a day over twenty. In fact, the company kept glancing at him, as if he were a younger brother away from home. René sat there, held in check by the others, with the beady eye of a viper intent on not missing a single word or detail.

As usual, it was as if René didn't exist. Not one of the partisans deigned to look at him; they saw him as nothing more than a pile of blankets. When the bottle had been passed around nearly full circle, and he should have been next, the dark-haired lad nearest to him sent it back in the opposite direction. Not one of them pointed out that the sick man may have wanted a drop.

They didn't waste time with explanations as to why they were there, which probably meant that they had met up before from time to time. Now that the woods were no longer buried under six feet of snow, they must have decided to go back to normal. The conversation was light-hearted. Rather than a meeting of partisans discussing the revolution, it felt like an impromptu party in the thick of the woods. When they fell on their food, the den was silent.

He was lying there in his usual corner, slightly turned away from them. They were excluding him and he was excluding them. It was a shock, then, when he suddenly heard a voice say, "How are you doing here?"

A strange pause followed. Nobody answered. Finally, he turned his head. Holding a chunk of bread in front of his mouth, he said, "Are you asking me?" He had no idea who had spoken.

Only one person moved: the boy, who was nodding. The rest of the band had suspended all activity except their breathing and their worried glances. René addressed the company: "They tell me I was worse off before."

The boy shaved a piece of cheese off a slab and put it in his mouth. "And how's your leg?"

René looked at the rise in the blankets covering the splint. "Tormenta says it won't ever be what it was before." He was tempted to tell them about the madman's tortures, but he bit his tongue. Something was clearly going on. The fact that everyone was sitting there frozen to the spot was an indication.

"Is your memory coming back?" another partisan asked.

He said neither yes nor no, which was a response of a kind.

At that point, the boy appeared to drift off for a bit, lost in thought. A vestigial smile flitted across his gaunt face. "Faina says it's funny how every time you have any dealings with us, you get banged on the head."

René didn't hesitate, "I don't know anyone called Faina."

One of the three regulars said, "He's lying. We need to find out why."

It gave René a start, which sent a jolt of pain coursing through him. "Me? Lie? What for?"

The boy didn't answer right away; first he studied the invalid for a good while. Finally, he said frankly, "Maciste, are you on our side?"

René instinctively sought out Tormenta, to see if he would support him. The big partisan stood there like a salt statue. René still couldn't quite take the fresh-faced lad's grilling seriously. "I know you picked me up after an ambush. You call me Maciste, but the name is new to me." He had to ask the rugrat, and did so adopting the expression of a grandfather playing along with a game, "How old are you?"

The kid answered without batting an eye, "Nineteen," adding, "a month ago."

René looked around as if to say, "Are you really going to let this big baby, who still stinks of mother's milk, give me the third degree?" He looked up at a wall of scowling faces.

One of the new arrivals piped up. René had only just noticed that he was missing a piece of his ear. "Are you playing around with us?"

"What do you mean? How could I—?" His voice ran out on its own and he didn't finish the sentence.

They sat there for a while, as if they were staring one another down at a border crossing. Then the boy took up his role as spokesperson again. He had evidently been entrusted with the task of getting information out of him. "We want to know about the villa," he said. "You should tell us everything you know."

René let out a sigh. "I'd love to."

"But you don't remember a thing."

"It's the beating, I—" Again, he dropped the sentence half-way through.

The boy hung his head. He looked sincerely sorry. The others looked as though they were under a spell; they didn't dare open their mouths, and not one of them took a bite out of their bread, however hungry they must have been. When the boy started speaking, he was still looking down at his boots, which were incidentally a bit too big for him. "The first time she talked about you, we didn't want to know. 'A town cobbler?' we said. Moreover, at your age? But she insisted. One day, she said, 'He's been at war his whole life.' In short, we were supposed to believe her, whatever the cost. In the end, we allowed ourselves to be persuaded."

Touching that nerve was worse than the crash that had brought him to this place. He forced himself not to move a muscle. He didn't even blink.

The boy looked at him. "You may be happy to hear that Ombra is fine," he said.

René's veins were on fire. All of a sudden, he felt as though they were hammering a nail into his throat.

The kid went on. "The men looked askance at her at first. Now they all agree: she's one of our finest. She's at the Gerfalco front." He paused for a moment, then started again. "Maciste, you've done a great job. Now it's up to us. But you need to trust us."

Tears were rolling down his face and he didn't care at all. Looking the boy straight in the eye, he gasped, "Are you Boscaglia?"

It wasn't a question.

3

Tormenta's long face told René everything: the guardian of the den couldn't stand seeing him chatting away to their leader, who had never done more than huff, puff, and moan with him. It was clear now what the task assigned to the ogre of the cave had been: to ascertain what kind of prisoner they had, and whether his time in a cell at the villa had embittered him to an extent that he had turned against the fight.

Boscaglia said it happened. Being imprisoned during a war was a challenge; solitude and worry could brainwash you. They were happy to celebrate the liberation of a comrade, but they needed to tread carefully. Some survivors of Nazi detention centers had been as unpredictable as stray bullets. They had given René time to regain his senses, but now they were there to prod him. The three partisans who always left the hideout at first light had been reporting on his progress to the people in charge.

They suddenly started behaving like old friends and René learned all their battle names: Corvo, Balìa, Gilera, Fomento. It turned out he wasn't the only one being looked after. Other prisoners who had survived the attack had been taken to shelters dotted around the mountains, where they had been celebrated, taken care of and, more importantly, kept under a watchful eye.

Telling his story was an act of mental calisthenics that required his memory to work overtime. René found it almost impossible to keep up with all the details as they continued to wriggle their way out of the recesses of his mind. Recreating in words the journey he had made, from the day the first prisoners arrived in town to that terrible night when they had dragged him out of his cell in the villa, was more exhausting than climbing a mountain. He would manage three steps up and then slide back down two, but Boscaglia never lost his patience. Unlike Fomento, whose task was to take notes in an exercise book with names and any juicy details.

He told them about the camp and how it was organized. They handed him a sheet of paper and he drew a plan of the wing where he had been held—as he did so, he felt as if he were retracing his footsteps the night that he discovered Anna was actually Maria. Absurd as it seemed, he hadn't realized until that moment that the giant he had first set eyes on with Mosca and Faina in Anna's apartment had not been in the army van with him. "He's talking about out big bear, Orso," Fomento said.

Boscaglia asked René to tell him more about the haunted prisoner strategy because it amused him no end. It had been an unimaginably effective secret weapon that had ultimately thrown the soldiers' consciences out of kilter and given the internees a sense that they were part of something bigger than each of them. Simone had been brilliant at introducing the idea to those family members he had befriended in the early days. The strategy had been effective, shattering the nerves of both the Nazi and the Fascist soldiers, but then came the night he had been dragged away.

When he got to the part where he had to describe Ciavatti's brutal treatment of a slack-jawed Mosca, he found it hard to go on. Fomento gritted his teeth and swore revenge, while Boscaglia simply lowered his head as if he were entering a world of his own, as he often did. René still had Alfredo and Michele, and—worse still—Simone, to cover. It was essential that he rendered justice to Simone's desire to contribute to the rebellion:

the young soldier had been willing to sacrifice his life to catch
the Germans with their pants down. He had been left at the
villa on his own, with prisoners who were anxious about being
transported and fearful about being caught behind enemy lines
once the Allies arrived. "We need to go and save him," René
kept saying, but Boscaglia didn't appear to take up the suggestion. Even when he pointed out the exact point of access,
as well as the position of the armory, the young leader was un-
moved. Attacking the villa was a plan that the higher echelons
of the revolutionary organization had considered many times,
concluding each time that it was too dangerous. They didn't
have enough rifles and they needed their men up in the mountains, not getting mowed down by machine guns. "What about
the bishop?" René asked, feeling he was perhaps crossing a line.
Fomento burst out laughing bitterly and spat on the ground.
"Galeazzi needs to make his peace with himself and then with
God," he said. Keeping one foot in the revolution and the other
in the regime had always been his specialty, since the days when
he used to boast he'd been arm-in-arm with the Duce during
the draining of the Pontine marshes. He might have had a strategy of his own, but the brigade's view was that he was a slippery
character who was impossible to pin down. The message he
had sent them before the first prisoner transport was a case in
point. The matter was discussed at length in the woods, but
some claimed it might be a trap and, in the end, they didn't take
any action. Now, as René related what Simone had told him,
the two partisans bitterly regretted not having exploited the so-
called "failure" engineered by the driver, who had no doubt
been appointed by the bishop himself. "So, who told you about
the prisoners?" René asked. "How did you know they were taking us away in the dead of night?" When Boscaglia answered,
René's head span. Shrugging, the young leader said, as if it were
obvious, "Rizziello. Who else?"

Once again, he found himself listening to a story that

resembled a fairy tale. The main character was the very same Maresciallo that Ercolani had put in charge of the prison camp at the very beginning. The very same servant of the Fascist government and spy-hunter who'd had René captured and handed over to the Germans. Rizziello had a son. It was impossible to know how exactly, but he'd made quite sure that there were no doubts about his boy; even the provincial governor was certain that the son had been recruited up north. The truth of the matter was that he'd been in the Resistance for some time, fighting in the woods. His battle name was Barros.

The agreement between the Maresciallo and the brigade was simple: his son was to be kept away from the action and, in exchange, he would send messages the partisans might find useful. He had been unable to do anything about the prisoner transport. Sabotaging their transfer would have exposed him to danger, not to mention the fact that he would also have lost face with Ercolani, who had the power to order another transit from one day to the next. The partisans needed the Maresciallo to carry on running the camp; they'd already had a setback when the Germans had taken over command of the garrison. The Maresciallo needed the same thing: from his position, he could monitor the partisans' movements while pretending he wanted to rout them at any cost. When, in fact, he'd been protecting them. To protect his offspring.

It was ironic that the accusation against René that had brought him to the bishop's villa—that he'd been sending messages to the partisans—was precisely what Rizziello had been doing all along. Since he didn't know what to do with the cobbler, he'd decided to keep him safe in the wing with the political prisoners. And then, he had apparently obeyed Ercolani's new, top-secret order, which had been to take everyone away and kill them, obliterating every trace of abuse. From what René was hearing now, it turned out that Rizziello was the one who had set him free. He may even be obliged to thank him one day.

The ambush of the army vans hadn't created too many ripples for the regional governor. "Except he was shitting lightning bolts," Fomento said. Ercolani had chalked it down to bad luck: armed insurgents on a recce in the woods had been served up the two vans on a silver platter and they had grabbed the opportunity. Two soldiers had died and four more had been captured. Boscaglia was quick to specify that none of these soldiers fit René's description of Simone.

During their conversations, they kept coming back to one point: Boscaglia couldn't believe that René had gotten himself arrested without a plan in mind. It was the one detail in his account that didn't square with the rest. There was nothing the cobbler could say except that it had seemed like the best way to reach Anna. Once he was inside, he would decide what to do next. And, indeed, he had reached her, though it wasn't her but another woman. Finally, he couldn't keep the question back any longer. He gathered his strength and, flushing bright red, blurted, "Does Anna know about me?" In his urgency, he had called her by her real name by mistake.

Boscaglia's face lit up. "In these parts, everyone knows about you," he said.

4

T he group stayed two days. René now knew that referring to the boy as the leader of the revolution was over the top; the fact remained, however, that at the age of nineteen, he'd been heading one of the partisan units active in those mountains. In his turn, he'd been subject to the rules of the brigade. Certain superiors had been trying to garner information about the villa in preparation for when the Allies took Maremma by storm. That would be the time to attack the villa. Until the Americans arrived, they had been told to focus on easy yet crucial objectives and continue to put the spanner in the Germans' works.

It all made perfect sense, but his thoughts went to Simone, trapped there in a uniform that would be a death sentence. René suggested a hundred ways of rescuing him and Boscaglia was sympathetic. He understood his concern, but it was unthinkable to risk twenty lives to save one.

When the group left, René would have liked to go with them. Anna had a lot to do with it, of course, but she wasn't the only reason. Being stuck on that straw mattress was driving him up the wall. He started calling for Tormenta's medical attention rather than begging him to stop, ordering him to let him cry out like an animal, as long as he got back on his feet fast. The big partisan wasted no time. It was almost as if he were getting his own back. Maciste had acted dumb with him, and then opened up like a storybook as soon as Boscaglia had arrived. "I'm pretty sure we shouldn't let the bone set wrong," the guardian of the den said. "You haven't moved all this time. The only way to straighten your leg is to break it again and set the splints properly." There was no guarantee that René would regain full use. Quite the contrary.

They did it one afternoon. Tormenta prepared him well, with a half-liter of wine and generous slugs of liquor. A blow to the head would have saved them the trouble, but Maciste was recovering from that injury, too, and they didn't want to treat his head like a radio that stops working after one too many thumps. As soon as Tormenta was satisfied that René was sufficiently warmed up with drink, he said, "Let's pretend you've been on a binge and have done with it." Tormenta was suddenly scared. He didn't want the responsibility of busting him up for good. But the invalid was determined. If he was going to be a cripple anyway, he may as well do something to try to improve his situation. The alcohol had given him Dutch courage. He would have done it himself if he'd been able to.

All Tormenta had to do was put his hand on René's knee from the side, tuck his patient's ankle under his armpit and give one forceful snap. That would do it. Let whatever needed to break, break. Once he had taken up his position, he said, "Count to three."

Without batting an eye, René obeyed the order. But nothing happened. After a moment's pause, he said, "So?"

"So, I can't do it," he heard Tormenta say.

René started guffawing drunkenly. "Come on! The sooner you do it, the sooner I'll get better."

Tormenta was paralyzed. The idea of breaking René's leg had drained all the color out of him. And yet he had boasted countless times of how he had emptied his cartridge on the enemy without any qualms. Killing seemed to have been easier for him than cracking a bone. Despite the drink, René said soberly and calmly, "If you don't do it, I'll be stuck like this for the rest of my life and it'll be your fault. If you do it, I'll thank you forever for having tried, come what may."

The pain was white, a shard of light illuminating the cave. He didn't hear the screams, but he knew he was yelling because, from one moment to the next, he had been reduced to just that: a voice in shreds. Tormenta's words were an accompaniment. "It'll get better soon . . . " he muttered repeatedly as he fiddled with getting the splints in the right position. When he tightened the first lace, the pain was even worse, but René didn't pass out. Then it was time for the belt, which Tormenta strapped around René's knee. As he gave a final tug to the buckle to reach the last hole, Maciste could feel a *snap* echoing through his body. He might have asked to be finished off. Clamping his ankle at that point was child's play. René was so absorbed by the pain that he almost didn't notice the final twist.

The flask was at his lips again, with Tormenta saying, "Knock this back," though he probably needed it more than René, who opened his lips and ended up choking on the drink. The coughing fit that followed added insult to injury. His vision was still blurred. "Breathe," the big partisan said, holding his head. "It's over now. Breathe . . . "

They both knew it was just the beginning. Thirty minutes later, real pain hit him like a sledgehammer. When their comrades got back from their daily patrol, they found him in a pool of sweat on the pallet, with Tormenta laying cold rags on his forehead to cool his rising fever.

They could do nothing but encourage him to eat and drink. Every breath cost him, and if the blanket shifted so much as an inch, he felt on the point of death. He couldn't even allow himself the luxury of screaming, unless he wanted to make the pain worse. He whiled away the time there in his corner, as still as a stone. The days had grown longer and, through the opening of the cave, he would watch as the light changed over the same, tiny segment of the world. The best time was towards evening, when the sun hit the split in the rocks. It was fleeting, but he would absorb the light while it lasted without narrowing his eyes. For ten minutes or so, he would let it shine on him like a caress and he began to feel it was like medicine for him. Then he would drift a little blindly into the darkness, until he heard the cry of a curlew.

He hardly slept at night. When Tormenta was not giving a concert with his snoring, he would tune in to the young partisans' breathing. They would fall into a deep sleep right away, and he would often find them in exactly the same position when they opened their eyes the next morning. Corvo was usually the first to get moving. After stretching a little, he would pull Gilera up, who would then proceed to wake the others by coughing. "Drop dead," was Balìa's way of saying good morning before heading out to take a piss. Passing by the mountain of blankets that Tormenta would bury himself under, he would give him a light kick with the tip of his boot. This would set off the grumbling of the den's ogre.

There were times when René felt a throb of happiness. And yet, they were living like animals in their filth, far away from everything, with every bite of food measured out. In his case, hunkered down at the back of the cave, things were even worse. The only thing that ever happened was an animal chancing upon them in the woods, or a sudden downpour. Tormenta had been renamed Torment, given his enthusiasm for shifting him onto one flank and then the other to avoid bedsores. The level of pain that afflicted him during these maneuvers was a measure of his recovery. After ten days or so, in fact, the black bruises were beginning to turn purple and blue, with garlands of yellow around them. The swelling had also gone down and the limb was beginning to take on the appearance of a leg, rather than that of a boiled ham. His guardian would often make remarks to coax him into laughter, "Maciste, you'll be waltzing out of here before you know it."

May arrived and he was still there: a spectator of the war. From deep in the woods, war looked almost easy. As long as

you got used to a certain kind of life. His days at the villa belonged to another era, but he would still occasionally take refuge
in thoughts about home. He would close his eyes and imagine
walking through the rooms where he had been raised. Incredibly,
there were details he couldn't make head or tail of. For example,
was that picture with the kids standing around the water fountain
hanging on the left or on the right of the fireplace? It had been
there for as long as he could remember. Anna was the biggest
shock: a suggestion, an intimation of her blondness, a trace of a
smile, a sound he couldn't reproduce. He would go over scene
after scene, but the contours of his dear friend escaped him; he
felt a rush of warmth to his heart instead. This made him chuckle
to himself: he had sacrificed himself for something closer to myth
than reality. The thought didn't displease him.

Staying put was agony when the fresh courage of so many
youths surged throughout the forests of Italy. He could tell
from the pallet where he was still stuck, and where he saw a
human wreck: maimed in his right hand and crippled in his left
leg. While out there, the wind of change was blowing, trum-
peted here and there by those young people who were weaving
the fabric of a new nation, which, like Edoardo, they may never
even see. It was the gift of those partisans in the prime of their
lives. That was what he thought, and looking back to the beginning of the adventure, just five months before, made him feel
mean-spirited. He had spent his life stooped over a senseless
existence, soaked to the marrow in the deception of a quiet life,
incapable even of embracing love. And that sentiment of love,
too, had slumped into an armchair and looked out of the window, numb with neglect, convinced it had been doomed from
the miserable start, to the point where it had said, "What's the
point in trying, nothing will ever change."

He could move his toes, even though when Tormenta touched
him it felt like he was being touched through a blanket. They
both knew more agony was on its way. If they didn't want his leg

to turn into a plank of wood, they needed to bend his knee. They didn't rush into it this time. They started slowly and, at first, René hardly realized he had moved it. The big nurse had suddenly developed hands of gold, brushing his kneecap as if he himself might be the one to break. A completely different story compared to the earlier tortures. Tormenta was committed, and had taken it as a personal challenge: getting Maciste as far as possible back onto his feet would be a kind of redemption after failing so badly in his initial task, which had been to find out what kind of man the wounded prisoner was. It would be a way to say to Boscaglia and the others, "It's not true that I'm useless." One day, he made his intentions clear when he came back into the den with a long, forked branch. He sat down, took out his penknife, and started peeling the bark off the hard wood. When René asked him what he was doing, he said, "Don't be an idiot. We need a crutch if we're going to get you walking, don't we?" Then he quickly changed the subject. "Bartolomeo Pagano," he said.

René didn't understand. "What?"

"The first time they told me about you, how could I not picture you as the giant in *Cabiria*?"

René felt as if he were trying to pick up the pieces of a conversation that had never begun. "Do you mean the film?"

"I'm forty-seven. All the kids in my time wanted to be a muscleman like him. When they told me your battle name, I cursed myself for not thinking of it when I had to choose one. I would have loved that name." Tormenta looked over at his invalid companion and gave him a cunning look. "Let's be honest: it doesn't suit you very well."

Tormenta got a little laugh out of him. "I was given it," René said.

At every slice of the knife, the big man grunted like a pig. "Then I got to know you better. And in the end I think it's a good name for you."

"Thank you."

"Think about it. What makes Maciste special?

René, too, used to like pretending to be that actor in his games as a child. Then he lost all his enthusiasm after the accident at the lathe. "For example, a lucky break," he suggested. "It's not every day that a stevedore gets to be a movie star from one day to the next."

Tormenta shook his head with irritation, as if a horse-fly had landed in his ear. "I mean the hero. I'm asking you, Maciste. What are your name-sake's qualities?"

The answer was easy, "His super-human strength." René added immediately, "In which case, I'm not remotely like him."

"What else?"

"He's tall, well-built . . . what are you getting at?"

Tormenta vigorously sliced off a piece of bark that ricocheted off the walls and then fell at his feet.

He put the knife down on his lap. "Super-human strength with a tender heart," he said. "In every film, someone kidnaps a woman and they call Maciste to rescue her. Just like you, right?"

René didn't have the chance to answer; there were noises outside. "Someone's there," Tormenta said, grabbing his rifle. He was in position at the mouth of the den in seconds.

Was it an animal? Soldiers didn't move around so quietly. Tormenta roared to himself, "Sons of . . . " Then he went out into the open, and lowered his rifle. "Hey, are you trying to get shot?"

The first one to come in was Corvo. He hopped straight into the corner where they kept the wine, like the crow he was named after, and slumped down with the flask to his mouth. Balìa and Gilera followed. They collapsed like their companion without saying a word. They dumped their bags and weapons as if they were being attacked by ants. Meanwhile, the guardian of the den had come back in, but didn't dare speak. Even more so, after Gilera had dropped his head in his hands and started to sob.

5.

C orvo spoke as if he were on the edge of a cliff. Rather than tell them what had happened, he sounded like he was trying to convince himself it was true. "Last night, Boscaglia left the Carline safehouse with five others," he said. "Their mission was to sabotage the power lines on the Pavone bridge . . . " He paused and then forced himself to go on. "At the first light of dawn, they were ambushed by the Fascists."

Balìa chipped in, "They managed to save Ciocco, but he's in a bad way. He won't make it through the night."

A precise question was swirling around in both René and Tormenta's minds but they didn't have the courage to ask. Corvo sighed deeply and put them out of their misery. "The only ones left are—" He was unable to finish the sentence.

Everything was silent. Even the noises in the woods seemed to have suddenly been hushed. Finally, Gilera broke the stillness. "He was shot in the leg during the struggle," he said. "He had stayed behind to cover the others; there was no way we could get to him."

Corvo went to comfort his comrade, who could hardly breathe. He spoke like a telegraph, "They tortured him to get names out of him. They didn't know who they were dealing with. Boscaglia suddenly snapped and managed to grab the rifle they had taken off him. He killed one of them. That was when they finished him off. He was buried on the spot."

It was impossible not to think of Edoardo. That despicable way of disposing of a body without even returning it to the family. Neither a word, nor a cold stone slab to kneel on. Canceled. Tormenta's expression was uncharacteristically fierce. He clenched his fists. "We need to go and get him, whatever the cost."

Balìa shook his head. "The Fascists changed their minds." Staring glumly at the wall of the cave, as if the scene was being projected there, he added, "They dug him up."

Tormenta gave a start. This appeared to have been the part of the story that had affected him the most, an unspeakable profanity he would not tolerate. "What?"

The words that came out of Corvo's mouth a few seconds later were too much for any of them, even the ones who already knew what had happened. For René, too, they were like a branding iron; he was tempted to plug his ears and shut them out. It wasn't just an account of how things ended: the poison would stay in him forever.

Boscaglia's body had been dug up and dragged along the road as far as Massa Marittima. As a warning to the inhabitants of Maremma. As they were speaking, pieces of that boy, whose battle name recalled the woods where he'd briefly reigned, were being strewn along the tarmac, clumps of his dried blood stormed by flies. What was left of his ravaged body was being dumped in the town square, in front of the church.

They felt equally offended, flayed alive like their comrade. The Fascists had been ferocious in tearing the flesh off him. People at war are killed, but these soldiers had broken the rules and done much more. It was treasonous, not on the field of battle but a betrayal of life itself. Reviling Boscaglia's remains had been an act against nature and everyone in the den knew it: a thousand lives would never suffice to sweep that street clean.

They were brokenhearted, and so was the whole battalion. But war did not care about tears shed for fallen comrades; units were simply re-organized. Not one evening went by without the latest developments being relayed by their brothers in arms. News was mostly about the front down in Rome, where the American Fifth and the British Eighth Army had united forces. They had already routed the enemy in the battles of Anzio and Cassino. Now they were fighting at the gates of the capital city, and the Germans were in danger of being surrounded. Radio bulletins repeatedly broadcast the superiority of the Allied Armies; there had been an insurgence of Resistance activity throughout Italy. They were in the thick of the woods, hundreds of kilometers away, but they could still feel the earth shaking under their feet. Boscaglia's death up there in the mountains would be a prayer card they would stick on their foreheads. Every action they took would be for him.

There was an ill wind for the Germans blowing in from the front and they were turning nastier than ever. There was talk of new outrages that yet again revealed the truth: they felt cornered. The roar of the enemy on the horizon was making them shit in their boots. The mood was perceived by the populace, who after a winter of extreme hardship, was beginning to raise its head again. According to his companions, more and more people were signing up with the partisans. Balìa despised them. "They've suddenly realized what side they should be on. If it were up to me, I'd send them back home with a kick in the ass."

Volunteers were rolling up even from Massa Marittima, where Boscaglia's tragic end was still on everyone's lips and in their hearts. Many of them had decided to head for the hills after witnessing the butchery. The Fascists had mangled a boy's body as a warning; the result was dozens of young men lining up to march up to the mountains at night. When describing the event, they invariably ended up extolling the courage of a young woman named Norma, a fearless combatant, who had joined the partisans right after the armistice of Cassibile. Throughout the long winter, she had sheltered runaways, raised money and supplies for the resistance, and procured weapons and ammunition. Norma had been the one to collect Boscaglia's remains. The only person to openly challenge the Fascists, put an end to the anguish of a body dumped in the square, and finally give him a proper burial.

René thought of Anna and the argument they had had back then, when everything had first started. He saw himself urging her strongly to leave all that madness to the insurgents and, once again, he was forced to accept that he'd been wrong. So many things had had to happen before he was ready to remove the blinkers he'd been wearing in Le Case. While he and his drinking partners had been throwing back shots at the Due Porte, the youth of Maremma had been risking their lives to bring about change. He had been so narrow-minded that not even Edoardo's death had opened his eyes to what was going on just outside the workshop.

Now that he finally *was* ready and willing to jump into the fray, he was stuck in that cave. He could barely put his foot down. That would be his battle. The partisans were preparing to cut off the retreating Germans, and he was struggling to stand upright. The day he managed to take his first step outside, he felt a flush of courage that made him fall into a hole in the ground; if Tormenta had not been propping him up, he would have been back to square one. "Hey, where are you running to?" he teased.

Having not used it for so long, his leg was thin as a rake, floppy, and useless. He could move it a little, but it didn't feel like it belonged to him; when it touched ground, he couldn't feel a thing. His exercise consisted in standing up, steady as a telegraph pole, with his weight on the crutch. He would be bathed in sweat in no time at all, without having moved so much as a muscle. Then Tormenta would take him back to his pallet and go out again on the lookout. Now that the front was beginning to move again, he once more had a part to perform. The cave was on the eastern face, which was very steep.

It was an excellent view point from which to see much of the Maremma, including a good portion of the plains, all the way to Montepescali. Tormenta wore his binoculars around his neck at all times. Every three hours, he would take out his mirror and send messages to his comrades on the next peak, who would answer him with more flashes. But neither lookout had anything to communicate.

Capturing Germans who were being forced to fall back as the Allies pushed the battle lines forward was no easy task. News came in of retreating soldiers committing atrocities, both on prisoners and on the population. Usually, before taking down their positions, soldiers received orders to clean up. Being gunned down by a firing squad, just days before coming under the protection of the Allied Armies, was the worst kind of humiliation. The Nazis were losing the war Nazi-style, leaving a trail of blood behind them.

By the time the matter of bishop's villa came back into fashion, it was already the beginning of June. René had often wondered how Ercolani was taking things. What would Monsignor Galeazzi have to say for himself? He could just see him standing at the gate, greeting the Americans with that saintly smile plastered all over his face. Would a blessing be enough to avoid arrest? And then there was Rizziello. It can't have been easy play-acting in that situation, supporting the partisans while keeping up a façade as a Maresciallo under the orders of a Fascist government. How far would he be prepared to go before handing himself over to the liberating army? Would he send the Maremma soldiers into battle? Simone was one of their contingent.

One item of news surprised them: there had been another transport. They had no idea how many families had been sent up north. It had taken place right under the noses of the partisan patrols, distracted by having to keep an eye on the retreating

Germans, and they had missed their opportunity. Balìa, as usual, was the most argumentative among them. He shrugged, unable to let go of the fact that there were no Jews in the woods fighting for the cause. "Why should I fight for them?" he said. One look from Tormenta was enough for him to understand he had said something stupid.

It was further confirmation, though, that the Allies had practically arrived in Grosseto. The governor of the province was keen not to leave behind any trace of the prisoners. In his message to the partisans, Rizziello had asked that they pay special attention to the next transportation. An evacuation order may arrive from one moment to the next, just as it had that night when a van full of prisoners had moved a cobbler out before his time. Corvo turned around and couldn't stop himself from looking down at René's leg. Then he held his gaze. "We're all going down tomorrow," he said. The partisan high command had made up their mind.

6

T he sun was already high by the time they left the hideout. Nothing happened to begin with; they were alone
in the middle of the woods. The younger partisans took
the lead, marching in an open triangular formation. Tormenta
and Maciste lagged behind, Maciste in agony, struggling to keep
up with them. He used the crutch as support on one side; on
the other, there was Tormenta, whose firm grip could support
his weight entirely when required. Suddenly, Balìa raised his
arm and they came to a halt.

René stood there looking around like the others although,
unlike them, he didn't know how to read the stirrings in the
woods. He wouldn't have been able to tell the difference between the sound of a wild boar fooling around in the undergrowth and that of a combatant. All of a sudden, he caught
sight of three of them.

They were walking in a loose formation, the middle one with
a rifle slung across his shoulders like a crucifix, his hands swinging loosely on each side. The man greeted them with a clucking
noise and Corvo responded with a nod. They continued their
descent.

Every now and again, he would look up and chance upon
posses of men on the march. The mountains seemed to be ooz-
ing partisans wherever he looked. They were coming out of
nowhere, as if they had just crawled out from under a rock. A
silent procession, mostly youthful, although some of the strag-
glers were even older than René. He felt better when he saw

that he wasn't the only wounded man finding it difficult to keep up the pace.

It took no longer than an hour to get down. He didn't say anything, but his leg was killing him. Tormenta noticed because René was leaning on him with all his weight and dragging the crutch along behind him as if it were a stick. They slowed down when they saw the rooftops of Le Case twinkling before their eyes.

The town lay there to their right, much of it hidden behind the slope of the mountain. If they found a good position through the trees, they could also see the valley. They stopped just before the glade that opened up suddenly and steeply over the road.

Tormenta handed him the water bottle; René was tempted to empty it over his knee to cool the burning sensation. "Now what do we do?" he asked.

Tormenta glanced at the other clutches of partisans who, like them, were regrouping. There were fresh young combatants stretching as though they had only just woken up. They were slinging their haversacks on the ground and clowning around as if they had decided to meet up there for a big picnic. Tormenta said, "We'll wait."

René leaned on a tree. Looking at Le Case, he could see the old part of the town that for thousands of years had soared up from the rocks like a ship riding the waves. Seeing it from that perspective was strange; it looked like a sleeping giant that he was watching over. Then, there was movement; Corvo and Gilera went to speak to the young partisans in the other squad, and that was when René spotted him. The second their eyes met, the other man turned away.

Mandela was sitting on a rock not too far off. René realized immediately that he wasn't a prisoner; in fact, he was wearing the partisan's red bandana around his neck.

He again had the feeling that the world had done a somersault:

before his eyes was yet another protagonist of the revolution, one he had not expected to see there. He hadn't seen a familiar face for months and was about to strike out and greet him, but then he looked more closely. The man's expression was a give-away. Despite his crumpled clothes, his fellow townsman didn't look one bit like a fighter worn out by long marches and hardship. His haircut didn't suggest weeks of stakeouts or any other clandestine task. René saw Mandela steal a glance in his direction, but as soon as he realized the cobbler was staring at him, he turned away.

His first thought was, "Poor Claudio." He was sitting there like a gatecrasher at a party. René had no idea what had led him to join what had been renamed the Guido Boscaglia Brigade, but even a blind man would be able to see from a great distance that he had nothing in common with the partisans. He would have liked to ask him, "When did you roll up to join the reds, then?" It couldn't have been more than two weeks. And what had happened to the lovely Loredana? Whatever, Mandela was squirming with embarrassment at being caught out there. Signing up with one of the partisan detachments in the woods to save his skin revealed his true colors. The gaze of a cobbler who knew his story was shredding him to pieces.

Corvo and Gilera returned to their group. Gilera was more emotional than his companion; he kept trying to dry his eyes, but couldn't stop crying. He was sniveling like a kid and René was convinced there was more devastating news. Instead, the young partisan said, "We've been liberated." Corvo was acting tough but his eyes were also glistening. "We're going home," he said.

7

They looked no different, he thought, to those human beasts that had arrived in town one day. Clutches of people continued to arrive from the alleys onto Via Roma looking lost. For some, the very fact that their boots were treading the sidewalk was a miracle; others would burst into tears in front of a store sign as if they were kneeling before Jesus.

The younger partisans marched proudly down the street, rifles slung over their shoulders, but even they were surprised when some old ladies started showering then with flowers from their windows. René saw a tank parked in St. Bastian's square, the soldiers helping the girls up onto the treads.

The partisans were like mice who had thrown open all the manhole covers and were coming from everywhere. Women threw themselves at the wounded, and he suddenly found himself the object of attention of Damiana Cocchi. "René," she cried, preparing to pull him out of the tight clasp Tormenta had adopted to drag him down the mountain. Suddenly, the big partisan looked as though he needed support: without a crippled companion to prop up, his emotions were so overpowering he risked falling on his backside right there and then.

There were so many tears, but they all added up to the biggest laugh ever. Young girls arrived with pots of water and glasses of wine. Both young and old, dressed in rags, fell to their knees and, instead of drinking, hugged the children. Corvo, Gilera and Balìa had disappeared without trace. In the crowd, René saw a handful of flaxen men being handed over to some soldiers. Two things became clear: first, the Americans were normal people; second, there were deserters from the Wehrmacht in the midst of the partisan bands. The merry-go-round in that particular circus linked together an unlikely variety of animals.

Tormenta continued to walk around aimlessly, as if he were intoxicated. All of a sudden, René tugged at him. The words he was about to utter felt impossible, but they came out of his mouth nonetheless. "I live over there."

Cesare Calò was sitting on the step by the front door of his building, his elbows on his knees and his head in his hands. He seemed to be attending a funeral rather than a celebration. His expression didn't change when he saw René. If anything, for a moment, it seemed like he was looking daggers at him.

"Cesare, it's me. Don't you recognize me?" he said. The other man looked as if he were gazing at him from the bottom of a well. "Where's Danilo?" As soon as he had formulated the question, he regretted it. He wasn't sure he wanted to hear the answer.

The boy popped out of the crowd at that very moment and flew to his father, looking as skinny as a sparrow. René sighed with relief. "Hey!" he said. Danilo answered with a lopsided smile, but there was something working inside him. René's thoughts went to Rosa but he decided not to enquire after her. He signaled to Tormenta to help him go inside.

Setting foot inside the entryway was like crossing the frontier of a dream. How could everything still be the same? He shot a glance at Anna's front door and saw that it had been smashed. There were leaves in the corridor and a turbid puddle had formed at the entrance. He pictured Anna coming down from the Gerfalco woods, and wondered whether the news had traveled that far. He realized that the idea of seeing her again wasn't giving him the usual head rush and concluded it must have something to do with the inebriation of his return. Although his feet were firmly planted on the floor tiles of his building, a big part of him was still up there in the woods, or even locked up in the bishop's villa. He thought of the hidden key amongst the stones that he no longer had any use for. He looked straight ahead and said, "And now?"

He meant the stairs, two narrow, badly-lit flights of them leading up to the door of his apartment. He had been running up and down those steps all his life, but the very idea of the climb now made him feel faint. He wasn't in time to grab hold of the banisters before the entryway suddenly turned on its head and he found himself staring at the ceiling. Tormenta had hoisted him up in his arms. "I've been thinking about this for a while," his big nurse said. "Renée is a woman's name, isn't it? Well, I'll carry you over the threshold like a new bride, but don't you go getting any strange ideas."

His feet touched ground again when he was on the landing in front of his door, which was also damaged and dangling on a hinge by a miracle. One look was enough to confirm the worst: not only had Rizziello's soldiers devastated the place, but a window left open for months had done the rest. Swallows had nested inside and were now flitting against the ceiling like bats. Tormenta chortled wheezily. "Maciste, compared to this, the den was a royal palace." They went in.

"Go on! Go and get yourself a drink!" René had repeated for thirty minutes, but Tormenta didn't like the idea of leaving him alone and kept himself busy tidying up the house. Straightening the table, all of a sudden, he looked deflated. He gave up the pretense he had been keeping up for no reason in particular and said, "I'm not ready, you know."

In short, after months and months in the thick of the woods, he was scared to show his face. That was why he was procrastinating. The idea of joining the crowds made him short of breath. Maybe he had gone mad. As innocent as a child, Tormenta said, "What if I've lost my mind?" He wasn't eager to jump on the first van heading in the direction of his own family on the Tatti side of the mountain. He didn't want to think about what he'd find when he got there. Would Margherita still be there? And what about Pietro, his handsome son who would be going on fifteen? "A war has just ended," he said. "I don't want to start a new one in mourning."

Maciste looked at him from his chair. During that endless string of days that they had spent in the den, he thought, Tormenta had never mentioned having either a wife or a child. He said, "If someone is waiting for you, it would be cruel to stay here."

The guardian of the den stood there lost in thought. He nodded, as though he were answering a host of questions. Finally, he gave one of his bull snorts, turned to René, and announced out of the blue, "By the way, my name is Valeriano Biancamaria."

René studied him, as if he were reassessing the big man in the light of that news. After a while, he said, "And you say *I* have a woman's name?"

They both burst out laughing.

It was enough for him to sit in his chair at the window. Finally, he could see something happening in the street. He didn't need anything else.

Via Roma had become an enormous street party. The old ladies who used to live in the building opposite were no longer there. Their absence was both good and bad, like when you decide to change pictures on a wall after a century. Meanwhile, army vans paraded by and detachments of partisans continued to rain down from the mountains. René would pick one random lad and follow his progress. He enjoyed watching their initial bewilderment. The mouths of some would hang open for minutes on end, as if to say, "Is this really how it all ends?" Then there were invariably hysterical scenes, ranging from desperation and crazy happiness, both of which could lead to unprecedented levels of rage, to weapons being thrown on the ground and walls in Le Case being pummeled. The first drunken songs had started.

Even his hunger had faded, and the evening breeze felt like a caress. René continued to wonder, "Did it all really happen?" He didn't mean the German's retreat. He meant the whole story. Was the whole thing a dream? Had he just woken from a nap? The answer arrived from his leg, but even that stabbing pain was not enough to assuage his doubts. Now that he was back home, being that person with the notebooks, in the villa, in the woods, felt impossible. His thoughts went to Edoardo. He heard himself mutter as he looked out at the celebrations, "I played a role, too." He caught sight of his reflection in the dirty glass that had captured the golden light of the sunset. Maremma had never seen anything as beautiful, that was for sure. He glimpsed a young partisan empty a flask of wine over his head then grab the first girl to pass by and start dancing without music. If that wasn't a revolution . . .

Every now and again, he would fall asleep, only to be woken by yells and the revving of scooters. He smiled as he recognized himself bathed in the light of the street lamp. It was late at night, but there were still people in the street. A long line of heads snaked along the sidewalks. At one point, a bonfire was lit. He heard feet squelching, then two knocks on the table. He turned.

In the shadow stood a figure.

Out of the blue, he heard the words, "What about a little omelet?"

TWENTY YEARS LATER

1.

When the weather was nice, he would enjoy a stroll in his lunch break. He would head out towards Sassoforte and, after he had passed the little statue of the virgin, he would stop in the square in front of St. Martin's and look back at Le Case.

He liked that best of all. From there, the town looked so beautiful it was heartbreaking. He realized one day that the miracle occurred because you couldn't see a single inhabitant of the town from that distance. He would say out loud, "Come on, just a little further, and then I'll take you back to the workshop."

Talking to his gammy leg kept him company; he treated it like a lap dog, especially when the weather changed and he experienced pain. He would hear it yap and he would respond in kind. "So, you're in the mood for a chat today, are you?" or "Don't worry, how could I ever forget you?"

He would sometimes walk as far as the bishop's villa. The garden was overgrown with brambles and high grass. The gate was rusty and the shutters closed, their slats dangling. The first thing he had to do was get around the wall.

He had no idea when they had erected it. There were two possible answers: back in '43, to stop people seeing what was going on at the Monsignor's residence when prisoners had been held there; or later, once it was all over, to forget what had gone on there. Whatever the answer, the wall still stood. In his mind, bricks and mortar embodied the spirit of those individuals he bid good morning and good evening to.

Once he managed to get past the wall of shame, he would walk up to the rickety railings and look towards the woods. Right there in plain view was the cement monster where a cobbler who'd been well into his fifties had counted out the days. It was like watching the ghost of his past. For all he knew, many people's pasts were coming to life, wandering along the corridors and in the common room of that silent, abandoned building. He would sometimes pick a wild flower and throw it over the fence. Then he would say to the lapdog grinding at his leg bone, "Okay, okay. We'll go back now."

Many years had gone by, but he still couldn't get used to the way Le Case had gone back to business as usual after the war. If he ever felt like taking a draught of poison, he would go into the Due Porte and sit at one of the tables for a while and look around. Maso would be behind the bar, with some old fogey from the past such as Evaristo Zoni. Mandela would only turn up on Sundays before lunch, dressed in his best suit. He would order a Campari and smoke a cigarette in a holder.

Or Leonilde Cacciaferri would pass by on her niece's arm. He remembered her cracking her whip. Now she was off shopping in pearl earrings with a giant gold crucifix around her neck.

René always stayed home on Liberation Day. All those scumbags hanging on the mayor's lips when he gave his customary speech disgusted him, especially because the villa was never even mentioned. Don Laura also avoided the subject in his weekly sermons. René would bang his fist on the table and Cesare Calò would hang his head, he, too, unable to explain the collective amnesia that had struck the town. "They're ashamed," Cesare would say. René would feel the dog's teeth crunching on his knee and get angrier. "They are without shame."

Not one article had been written about it. It was as if the events at the villa had never taken place. In contrast, Monsignor Galeazzi's grand gestures were all over the papers: after the war, he created new parishes throughout the Maremma diocese and erected the immense cathedral of the Sacred Heart of Jesus. "It's guilt," his neighbor muttered. René didn't mind at all the idea that the bishop was still tortured by the echoes of those ghostly howls. Small mercies. But the fact that the chancery had given the contract for building all those new churches to the same engineer who had designed the prison camp at the villa was yet another slap in the face for him. Wars came and went, but business was business. Post-war reconstruction had made the old boys' network even greedier.

These days, they would meet upstairs in the evenings, but, every now and again, Cesare would knock on René's door at some unexpected hour with a bottle in his hand. Seeing him at the door warmed René's heart, as he relived certain desperate scenes when things had been the other way around.

A few words about his day and about Danilo, who had completed his studies and moved to Siena. Cesare still felt dizzy at the idea that his son had not only become a lawyer, but had also married a girl called Clara. After two glasses, however, they would fall into the usual black hole.

They would ask the same old questions until they both got a headache. Where had everyone gone? Where were the partisans, or the Maremma Jews? They had vanished after the war. Weren't they offended by the silence? René would sometimes try to bring the subject up, but the townsfolk would erect a wall as high as the one surrounding the villa. For example, when he went to pick up a prescription for his anti-anxiety medication, he would stare at the doctor as if to say, "Why don't you ever ask me about the prison camp?" Or else he would try to strike up a conversation about the tourists booked into the Bel Sole hotel for a few days. As these families walked by, he would hear complaints from other artisans and storekeepers. Foreign customs or traditions were frowned upon in Le Case, only to be forgiven when they rang up a fat bill in a restaurant and instantly became fast friends of the whole town. "There's no such thing as a free lunch," was the rule in those parts. When he saw those droves of new faces on the loose in Le Case, he would come out with something like, "They remind me of the people who came here in '43, though they are much happier, God forbid!" Any local at close enough range would clamp their mouths shut and leave immediately.

"Guilty conscience," Cesare said. Of the two, Cesare tended to be the one who looked carefully at things, searching for answers he could understand; he had already decided a while back that eating his heart out would get him nowhere. "Well, what happens, happens, and you don't lift a finger. Then everything ends and how do you return to normal? You need to find a way to look at yourself in the mirror. So, you make a silent pact with the others and decide that nothing happened."

René would answer his neighbor's explanations with the same old question. "What about the memory of those young men who got themselves killed? Claudio Montalti goes out for an aperitivo, strutting like a carabiniere, as if nothing's wrong. They haven't learnt a thing."

Their conversations would lead nowhere but, if the wine was poured out judiciously, at least they would stay within bounds. Occasionally, however, especially if the grappa bottle had been passed back and forth, they would go too far. René would throw back the last dregs of the shot glass. His watery gaze would suddenly explode with dismay and he would say, "God, I miss her."

Cesare would try to say something and fail. That was the way things had gone and there was nothing to add. He would usually chime in with memories of Rosa, his wonderful wife who had not made it through the terrible hardships of '44. Wars were never just bombs; there was always another hidden struggle within the families. Prolonged starvation took its toll on the fiber of those least prepared for sacrifice; for some, going beyond the limits God gave us made it hard to go back. That was what had happened to Cesare's wife. Dr. Salghini had been more specific: an iron deficiency had been fatal for Rosa Calò —she had gradually fallen into a coma and died.

René had one explanation only for why he hadn't gone mad with grief: Anna had died a happy woman. He remembered little about her illness and yet she had been unwell for months. He saw himself reading a book to her, or carrying her supper to her on a tray. Endless hours holding her hand. Doretta Mantovani coming every morning to wash her.

He had another strategy for getting over her absence. He would say to Cesare, "For me, she's still up there in the woods." Light-headed with drink, his heart swollen with emotion, he would add, "I'll be joining her up there some time soon."

At least Anna had had the chance to fight for Edoardo and for Italy. She had taught a lowly cobbler, too, who felt his friend was more alive than ever, even after her death. In fact, he never went to the cemetery. Instead, he would take his walking stick and set out for the villa. The final straw for René was the street name in Le Case, which had never been changed. There it was:

VIA DEL SEMINARIO

People continued to walk up and down the street as blithely as if they were picking poppies.

2

T he bell on the door of the workshop rang. He had been
working on Evelina Costagli's clogs: as usual, buying
a new pair would not have put her out of pocket, but
she was determined to keep these ones going, even though they
were the shape of a potato and the soles were worn through and
came unstuck every three months. He looked up.

A man he had never seen before stood at the door. He was
wearing a red, polo-necked sweater and had a thick salt-and-
pepper beard.

"Good morning," the cobbler said.

The man said nothing in return. He stood there with his
hands in his pockets looking like a mummy. He appeared to
be looking from a great distance. Finally, he mumbled, "Ciao,
René."

After a moment's hesitation, René dropped the pliers he had
been holding in his good hand.

Simone had grown up. Settebello couldn't stop staring at
him; he simply couldn't match the appearance of the boy he
had known with the man standing in front of him. And yet, it
was undoubtedly Simone: he blinked just as furiously, though
his voice had deepened a little. He had also filled out a good
bit, compared to the skinny young soldier he had been back
then—but he was still a good-looking fellow, considering he
was forty-three.

The door was locked. The flask with myrtle liqueur he kept

hidden behind the counter was on his work counter. René and Simone perched on the wobbly stools. They were feeling pretty shaky; all those years, and there they were, together again. The cobbler's head spun. More importantly, he didn't know how to interpret the impromptu visit. Did it bode well, or was he bringing bad tidings?

Simone told him how he was doing. In '64, twenty years after their cataclysmic experience in the prison camp at the villa, he had a wife called Cristina and a son who was nearly twelve. When René heard the boy had been christened Michele, a twinge of pain shot through his bad leg.

Maybe he could have saved them the question he asked, but the improvised get-together was killing him, and he came straight out with it, trying not to be rude. "What are you doing here?" There were a thousand other questions lurking behind that one, the most pressing one being, "Why haven't you shown your face for twenty years?"

Simone shuddered, as if a ghost had run a finger down his spine. He suddenly looked overcome. He said, "It's like after an accident: if you don't get straight back behind the wheel, you may never drive again."

René caught a glimmer of the old Simone. He tried to imagine what it must have been like for him after his time at the prison camp. He had seen demobbed soldiers in town who had waged a very different war once they were safely back home. They would spend days on end sitting on their front doorsteps in a stupor, or drinking beyond any human capacity. René said, "Nobody knows what happened at the villa after the Americans arrived. Nobody has ever said a thing, except that there was a shooting match and a few casualties." Forcing himself, he added, "I always thought you'd been one of them."

His words sounded almost like an accusation. For years, René had consigned his memories of Simone to a place in the afterworld and then, from one day to the next, there he was. He could see why he had come: a room that had been locked up for too long needed to have the cobwebs swept away.

Simone started talking suddenly; it was like a slap in the face that made both their heads spin from the giant leap back in time. "No good news was coming in from Grosseto," he said. "Sure enough, Ercolani had raided the cash drawer and done a runner. I followed orders but everything was a blur. Our main activity was to destroy documents. And then there was the big question of what to do with the prisoners still in the camp."

René acted as if he was ready to dip back in. "Well, we talked about that—"

"When the next lot of Jews was supposed to be sent up north, the bishop gave Calcagni a bag of sugar. He told him to stick it into the gas tank of the bus. The Fascist even asked me to watch his back. I was dreaming with my eyes open: more and more subversives were coming out into the open. While before, it had been no more than talk, all of a sudden I was seeing them in action."

Opening the gates of the past was not easy. "So, Galeazzi was really on our side?" René said softly.

Simone shrugged. "Who can say? He was starting to get his act together, given that the Allies had maybe passed Orbetello. Was he waiting for the right time? Or was he making sure he had witnesses who would speak out in his favor? I never understood. He knows. And God knows. Then another transport was being prepared. When the Germans came to check up on us, the bishop told them that the thirty prisoners had already been driven away, but in fact he had let them run away into the woods."

"As easy as that?"

"I thought they had all gone crazy, especially Rizziello, who suddenly lost his sight. From one moment to the next, you could take a prisoner to the gates of the camp right under his nose and he would look the other way. The only thing he cared about was that all the archives should be burnt. Then, one fine morning, I woke up and there was no trace of a German anywhere. Poof! They were gone. That was when the real war started."

"What do you mean?"

"We soldiers in the Maremma contingent were not all the same."

"I know that very well."

"A whole bunch of them were devoted to the Fascist cause and were ready to take up their positions. That vermin couldn't admit they had been fighting on the wrong side, alongside the thugs. The villa must have messed with their brain. I've thought about it long and hard and, ultimately, I think that playing at being prison guards gave them a taste of power. The war had given them purpose. With the Americans at their door, they risked losing that crumb of significance, and they couldn't accept it. Or maybe they were just bastards. They tried to lord it over those of us who were less zealous by nature. Passini picked on me. He had a sixth sense and could tell I was ready to go the other way. One day, he handed me a pile of papers and ordered me to throw them into the barrel and burn them, sheet by sheet. As I fed them to the flames, he watched me closely. Then the alarm was raised: three soldiers in our contingent had vanished. They had run away into the woods. Giacomo Passini flew into a rage. He found two of them and followed them. He reported back to Rizziello a few hours later with blood all over his uniform. It turned out that he had called out to them in the woods and pretended he wanted to escape with them; as soon as they lowered their guard, he'd finished two of them off. The third had gotten away. All hell was about to break loose with the Allies at the gates, and all he could think about was getting a special mention from the Maresciallo for killing fellow soldiers in cold blood."

Silence fell. Dwelling on those days was hard for René. He saw himself on that stinking pallet in the thick of the woods with Tormenta.

"Rizziello sent out the order: we were supposed to greet the Allies with our hands raised and our weapons at our feet. The die-hards were not happy; they looked scornfully at anyone who doffed their rifles. Then there was the other issue. The Maresciallo never actually said it in so many words, although it was pretty obvious. That is, if we wanted to go, we were free to do so. That is, if we took the risk of stumbling into blood-thirsty partisans on stakeouts in the woods. That was how it was: Americans ahead and partisans behind. Add to the mix the fervent fans of the Duce. The first shots came from them. I saw them telling Fiaschi off, after he had come down from the sentry tower. Then they arrested him. Rizziello looked on, like everyone else, but what could he do? He couldn't tell his soldiers off for punishing a deserter; it would have been an unpardonable offence, and would have triggered an instant rebellion. Those of us conducting the silent revolution also had our hands tied: if we had fired a shot against the Fascists, it would have set off a bloodbath. The liberating army would have arrived at the villa and found everyone dead amidst the stench of burnt flesh. Whoever felt they belonged to one side or another advanced or retreated in baby steps. The seminary garden was like a chess board with each soldier representing one of the pieces; some white, others black. A raised eyebrow on the wrong side was enough to cause a finger to reach for a trigger. We spent almost half a day like that, stuck in a trap. Meanwhile, we saw farm workers walking by. The front had arrived without a shot being fired. The only sign was people stepping out of their homes. Then there was a rumble of engines and tank treads. There was black smoke coming from the barrels. Rizziello was standing there in front of the villa, with his weapon at his feet. As soon as he saw the column advancing, he was the first to raise his hands. But Passini had a different plan. I saw him get on one knee. Then he hoisted his rifle onto his shoulder and started shooting at the Americans. Others followed suit.

René's only comment was, "Good God."

Simone was on a roll, and didn't even hear him. "The Allies' response was immediate: Tardelli's brains were blown out without even a warning shot. I saw Musetta drop, too, ending up on his backside. Meanwhile, others of us in the contingent, including me, were obstinately keeping up Rizziello's position: our hands lifted in surrender. We were crying our eyes out, keeping them shut tight. Ivano Collaveri broke the spell when he took his gun out, turned his back on our liberators, and started shooting at the Fascists in our lines."

The lump in his throat took Simone by surprise and he had to stop to take a deep breath, blinking furiously all the while. Then he started again. "Very few of us had ever killed anyone, me included. We found ourselves in the middle of a shootout: suddenly where you stood counted for something. No more pretending. We started screaming what we thought, not only about the war but about life itself. I must have sounded like a stuck pig as I took aim and fired at boys with whom I'd spent months and months patrolling the perimeter. I shot D'Antona in the knee. Then I realized that Colella had me in his sights and had decided to empty his whole cartridge on me, but all I heard was the thwack of bullets. I felt like I was in a bell jar. I killed him on my second attempt, even though my sight was blurred by tears. Suddenly, it was over. The garden fell silent. I realized I was still pulling the trigger, but I was shooting blanks; my ammunition had run out a while before. The moans of the wounded started, mingled with the Allies' orders as they invaded the camp. The Maresciallo was the first to be captured. Not many of us were still standing. We were squaring one another up like terrified children, unable to take in what had just happened. When I noticed Giacomo Passini, I was probably on the point of passing out. He was running towards me, with a knife, his face was contorted with rage. I stood there in a daze, shooting blanks, my arm limp and my pistol hanging at my side, and I was ready to submit to his fury. But something happened."

"What?" René gasped. It might have been minutes since he last drew a breath.

Simone sighed, as if he still couldn't really believe what he was about to say, despite all the years that had gone by. "Out of the blue, his right boot opened up like a slipper and Passini tripped; he was so intent on getting to me that he took a nose-dive to the ground. He quickly got himself back on his feet, but a shot felled him a few paces away from me. Immediately afterwards, someone caught me from behind. My gun was taken away and I fell to my knees.

3

Cesare Calò had been saying for years, "I know you're attached to it, but it's still an investment, isn't it? You could get something out of it." René would nod because his neighbor was right, of course. Pretending to think about it for a minute, he would always end up saying, "I'll leave the hot potato to you," and they would both have a little chortle.

After Anna's death, buying the apartment on the ground floor had been almost an imperative. Nobody, not even a distant relative, had shown up to claim it, so a price that a cobbler like him could afford had been negotiated with the town council. For almost twenty years now, everything he earned had gone straight into a savings account.

But he loved those moments when he took it into his head to go downstairs. He would search for the hidden key between the rocks. As he opened the door, he would say under his breath, "Can I come in?"

He hadn't changed a thing. If anything, when he had to call a workman in to make any repairs, he would feel sick to his stomach. Bringing the Maggi brothers in to decorate had nearly driven him mad; likewise, it gave him a stab of pain when he had to replace the old skirting board because of rising damp. The only thing René did was clean. He would take a moist cloth and polish corners, picture frames, or the shelves of the dresser. Then he would put the doilies his friend had crocheted back in their place. He never opened the bottom drawer, where Anna kept her personal papers, and he only ever stepped into the bedroom to tidy up. He spent most of his time at the kitchen table.

Everyone in town knew he had bought the apartment; there were sure to be people gossiping about how Settebello had lost his mind over a long-lost secret lover, who happened also to have been a partisan. On December 7, he would always buy a slice of chestnut cake and wash it down with slugs of wine until the flask was empty.

He used the apartment as a place of refuge, where he could return to a time when he had felt truly alive. It may have been just an impression, but when he stepped over the threshold the dog grinding at his leg bone seemed to let go for a while. He would tell Anna things about his day, which were nearly always the same. After Simone had called in, he couldn't wait to bring her the news. He settled into the chair and said, "Guess who came in today?"

He told her about the impromptu visit and how it had nearly sent him over the edge. Just talking about it made him feel as if he were in a dream, for one reason in particular: the way events had turned out owed a great deal to a very determined woman. René's secret weapon, the boots, had saved a young man's life. Without being nudged into a revolution, René would never have used the tools of his trade to fight his war.

Simone had turned out to be a good-looking man with a family. After their experience at the villa, the days had continued to roll by for both of them.

Simone had told him even more incredible things. For example, the Horsefly Game, as the man who had rung the workshop bell that day—whom he never would have recognized— had called it.

The game consisted of tracking down criminals. Once he had found them, Simone would go and sting them every now and then, even though the law considered them rehabilitated and they had been released from prison early. Take Ercolani, for instance: the man had been captured, tried, and sentenced to thirty years after the fall of Fascism, but he had only served seven of them. He had gone back to Bomarzo, his home town, in the province of Viterbo. Simone would take himself off on a jaunt. He hadn't been surprised to find that there was a legendary site nearby called the Monster Park. He had also hunted down Ciavatti, among other ignoble characters, and knew his address.

The Horsefly Game was easy: all he had to do was tail the delinquent, without doing anything else. Simone would follow them to the bar, down the street, or into restaurants. He would keep his distance and stare. Preferably on a special occasion. A daughter's wedding is a wonderful celebration, but at the end of the day, you'll notice a pair of eyes on you. You'll turn around and drown in a well; from that moment on, it will be impossible to ignore those eyes, which throw all your sins back in your face. Not to mention the suspicion that they are seeking revenge. It could take place at any moment. A fork suddenly dropped on the floor may sound like the crack of a gunshot, while those eyes vanish. Going to the carabinieri with an accusation of harassment would mean awkward subjects being brought up. Accusing the harasser then and there would be even worse, as certain details the family shouldn't really hear about may come out into the open.

Simone's new hobby was to kill war criminals slowly with his gaze. He never missed a single inauguration of a new church where Galeazzi was doing the blessings. He went to granddaughters' birthday lunches, christenings, and Good Friday processions. He would turn up at cocktails. He was the character standing there smoking at the water's edge while you were on vacation at the beach.

René knew one thing and one thing only: that if Anna hadn't flown the coop one day to go and join Boscaglia's band of partisans, none of this would have happened. Sitting at her kitchen table, he could finally see the blueprint of events that brought everything back to this place, where it had all started. He poured himself another drop of wine, but didn't drink it. He stuck his good hand into his pocket at pulled out a piece of paper.

It had been his project for the last few years, but he'd never found the courage to put it into action. He couldn't count the number of evenings he had spent contemplating those papers. Writing a will is not something you do from one day to the next. New things always come up, little things to reconsider. He always ended up putting everything away. "No, this time I'll go through with it," he told himself.

4.

The Anna: a low rise with a T-strap, pointed toe, eight-centimeter square heel. Inner and outer sole in leather, gold buckle.

Angelica Donati was the first person to stop in front of the window, looking for shoes for her aunt's wedding. She walked in and tried them on. She liked them so much, she decided to keep them on so that she could show off a little in town.

When the young woman left his workshop, René stood at the door and suddenly felt like smoking. Watching the beautiful Angelica walk away, he thought that maybe even in Le Case, people were finally ready for new shoes.

AUTHOR'S NOTE

Grosseto holds an unusual honor: during the entire period of the Holocaust, it is the only diocese in Europe to have signed a legally binding rental contract for a prison camp. Between 1943 and 1944, a hundred or so Italian and non-Italian Jews destined for the extermination camps were held prisoner in the Roccatederighi seminary.

When the Allies freed the villa, they found almost nothing. All the material regarding the prisoners (how many there were, which families, etc.) and the documents detailing the bishop's role had disappeared. The surviving papers are incomplete and only allow a partial reconstruction.

Historical research has brought the journey the prisoners were later taken on to light. After leaving the bishop's summer residence, they were transported to Fossoli, near Carpi, in the province of Modena. From there, they were taken north, mainly to Auschwitz. According to the archives, thirty-eight people were deported from the detention center at Roccatederighi, including eight children, one of whom was a newborn baby. It is likely there were more. One annotation reads, "Edith Singer, adolescent. Literally vanished into thin air."

The story of the wall is real. It is still standing, inside and out. I have taken a great deal of information from a book by

Ariel Paggi, *Il muro degli ebrei* (Belforte Salamone, 2018). In his introduction, the author recounts his struggle to glean direct witness statements. There was a wall of silence raised by those who could have spoken out and never did: "An entire community was loth to criticize a bishop's actions." Paggi adds, "Several local institutions contributed to consolidating the wall of silence."

The painful stories of the prisoners who were held there came out later. At the end of the war, survivors of the prison camp struggled to rebuild their families and eke out an existence having lost all their possessions. Their imperative was to forget and move on with their lives. Many Jews never told their stories, not even to their children. Paggi writes, "Still today, one witness, in the name of solidarity, deliberately omits the name of the spy that could have had him sent to an extermination camp in order to protect the man's descendants."

The Justice Ministry and the Ministry of the Interior minimized the events that took place at Roccatederighi. The prefect and the police chief both claimed that there were no *salient episodes* to be denounced and that there had been no *appreciable* reduction in the number of Jews residing in the province of Grosseto.

There are several police cases and judicial procedures against individual Fascist party members during the period of the Italian Social Republic. Having served as a prison camp guard was not considered a crime.

During the trial against Fascist leaders in the province, including Alceo Ercolani, for setting up and managing the Roccatederighi prison camp (as well as for transporting Jews to the extermination camps) no charges were made. In over eighty pages of transcripts, there was not one mention of responsibility.

The amnesty did the rest. While some leaders received severe sentences, most of them never spent a single day in prison.

The determination to consider crimes against Jews as minor

transgressions was borne out in the post-war period. Monsignor Galeazzi had no qualms in asking the Italian State to reimburse the rent that Ercolani had failed to pay for use of the villa.

In his book, Ariel Paggi tells the story of one hundred and seventy-four Italians from the province of Grosseto who were deported. Seventy-five of them had been imprisoned in the Roccatederighi camp.

Thank you, Ariel.

My book recounts this history through the eyes of a cobbler. The choice was deliberate, out of respect for the men, women, and children who were actually imprisoned in the bishop's villa. It was, of course, tempting to shed light on details of one particular family or another, but concentrating on one family would have meant ignoring all the others. In the end, I decided to rely on another device in my toolkit: evocation. I created a story that was close to many people's experience and that attempted to answer a simple question: what would happen if, from one day to the next, a prison camp opened right next to your house?

I was looking for my little *Pereira Maintains* in Maremma (those in the know will have picked up the reference to Tabucchi's novel in the herb omelet). Enraptured by a dream of love and redemption, René throws himself into battle and ends up reluctantly reshaping his view of himself and the world around him.

Settebello sees things, touches on things. He's "in the thick" of "a private matter," as Fenoglio entitled his partisan novel. Ultimately, he is on the edge of the action, and either passes unnoticed or is considered mad. Many accidental heroes of that war suffered the same destiny.

As we know, it took sixty years to establish an International Day of Commemoration in Memory of the Victims of the Holocaust, and the word "holocaust" has slowly filtered into the collective conscience. In the end, it was decided by international consensus that what happened in the extermination camps was worthy of commemoration. A form of collective guilt for which humanity will always have to ask forgiveness.

A commemorative plaque was placed in the garden of the bishop's villa on January 27, 2008. The inscription reads, "Numerous Jews, victims of racial persecution ordered by Fascism, were imprisoned in this place, partly transformed into a concentration camp between November 28, 1943 and June 9, 1944."

Other words of sympathy follow, with a plea never to forget. The first signature is from the GROSSETO HISTORICAL INSTITUTE OF THE RESISTANCE AND THE CONTEMPORARY AGE. The second, the DIOCESES OF GROSSETO.

* * *

Today is Thursday, February 10, 2022. An article in the newspaper reads, "Grosseto. A new square dedicated to Monsignor Paolo Galeazzi inaugurated today."

The mayor, Antonfrancesco Vivarelli Colonna says in a speech that he is proud that the Foibe massacres, in which Fascists were killed, were honored on the International Day of Commemoration. He ends his speech by stressing how important it is to recognize the dignity of human life.

* * *

April 25, 2022. The same mayor leaves the official festivities for the Liberation of Italy from Nazi-Fascism, saying he has other commitments.